Desired By Two

By

LaToya Johnson

My Time Publications
PO Box 49351
West Carrollton, OH 45449
www.mytimepublications.com

ISBN 10: 0-9820530-5-3
ISBN 13: 978-0-9820530-5-8
First Printing 2009
Library Congress Of Control Number: 2008944064

Printed in United States of America

10 9 8 7 6 5 4 3 2 1

Acknowledgements

Father, God, you are my everything. Thank you for the many blessings in my life. Even though, I'm writing these kind of books, I still thank the Lord. Without him, none of this would be possible.

Babe! My babe, my husband, my biggest fan! Thank you for being there for me. I couldn't have went on this journey without you. All my books still would've been sitting on the shelves collecting dust if it weren't for you. Thank you for believing in me. I love you so much!

My lovely angels, Alexis, Jonai, Osirus, and Heaven. Mommy loves you, and as always, this ones for you.

Mommy, I love you, and I never thank you enough for all you've done for me. Everyone wishes they had a mother like me.

Mando, you are the greatest. The best stepfather there is. I love
you.

Vera, my favorite step mommy! Hopefully my only. Dad, I love you.

Okay, to all my sisters, Raquel, Tia, Bria, Jerika, Jessica, Aliyah.

My sisters Delana and Brittany, thanks for being my biggest fans from the beginning!

To all my brothers, Denzel, Corey, Demetrius, Julius, Tavaris.

All my beautiful nieces, and nephews. Auntie loves you guys!

To my heroes, Grandma Mae, and Grandma Ethel. The most strongest women I know!

To all my Uncles, Aunts, cousins. All you are loved

by me. Of course you know that cause I give all ya'll much love!

A special thanks to all my relatives in Utica, New York! I miss ya'll too much!

Another special thanks to my relatives in Fremont, Ohio! I still don't see many of you guys. I miss you too!

To the friends that love me, and to the friends that hate me. Ya'll cool too!

To everybody that looked out for me on "Murder was the Case".........(Just to name a few)Melissa Sandwisch, Maribeth Taylor, (besides you two supporting my book, thank you for never doubting me, and being friends always! Love you guys so much!) Janet Sheffield (love you),Mary Freeman (love you), Al Darling, Jackie Jones (RIP, love you too much!), Melissa Kidd (love you), Lisa Burel (love you), Anna Garza, Maya Peacock (love you), Shawn Reed, Monique Stovall (love you, and miss you), Russell, Steve (Boonie), Ken (Junebug), Jack Clingmenton, and all kinds of family! oh geesh....I know there's more.....cause I signed so many of them. There is a couple I don't remember your name, but you are very appreciated. People like you guys that actually go out and support an author. That's very special, and it means a lot. To all my new fans, thank you for loving me! If I missed you, and I signed your book personally, I am truly sorry. I thank you too!

Thanks to Leila Jefferson for inspiring me in every way! Since I met you, I think I read your biography just about everyday. (sounds crazy, but true) You are one of a kind, and the best editor ever!!!! Thanks for seeing something in me.

A special thanks to, uh.... I don't even know your name. Everytime I see you, you inspire me with your words. You tell me good things that I want to hear. Thank you for loving my book, and giving me the best compliments ever. You'll know who you are, cause I'll run into you again. I always do!

And again, to everyone that stood by me, I love you guys, and I'm so glad I have your support. I mean that from the bottom of my heart!

Love,
Latoya

Desired

By

Two

Prologue

I stood in the middle of the airport, not wanting to be there. My heart was still broke, and probably would stay broke for quite some time. I met Quentin when I was fifteen years old. He was my love. Ten long years we were together. Ten long, stressful years, but I still loved him. I knew he loved me, too.

The last time we were together I had just forgiven him for cheating on me. I could never stay mad at him long, no matter how hard I tried. Now, he would never be back, and I was mad as hell at him for living this secret life. I had to find out about it from the strangers that murdered him. Those mutherfuckers came into our home and tortured Quentin. My helpless ass was in the bathtub, not wanting to come out. But what was I to do? If I came come out they would have killed me, too. The gun was in the closet in our bedroom, and that's where they all were. I heard it all from the moment they came in. I could hear Quentin telling them he was the only one there. He wanted me to stay quiet and not be seen.

"Where's the fuckin' money?" That was a question they were asking a lot.

Quentin wouldn't reveal where it was. I didn't even know where it was, except the chump change. Were they talking about that? Quentin was a drug dealer, but not big time. We had a safe in the house, which held $15,000 and that wasn't shit! When I first met him he was the big Willy, making $15,000 in a day. Quentin told me he was laying low for a while and that's what he did. If them guys came for the $15,000, why wouldn't he tell them where it was? Why did he die for $15,000?

While we made love that night he told me we had to leave town for awhile. Were these guys the reason he wanted to leave? Quentin was doing some other illegal shit that I never knew about. I didn't even want to know. All I wanted to do was get the hell out of New York.

When I heard the shot go off that ended my baby's life, I slipped into the linen closet in the bathroom. They knew someone else was in the house so I hid deep in that closet. I could hear the guys rambling around looking for me, calling out two names.

"So which bitch are you?" he says. "Sonya or Azaria? One of you bitches gonna die right now." I was terrified. "I bet its Azaria. You're the main bitch, huh? You shoulda been with me! You don't know shit anyway, baby, so I ain't gonna kill you. He kept you clean. If it's you, Sonya, I'll do you like I did Quentin. I heard you was the dirty bitch. You robbed me!"

Then, another guy spoke. "Let's burn this bitch!"

Those were the last words I heard, and then I thought it was over. It was far from over, because a couple minutes later I was choking. Choking from the smoke. Them mutherfuckers actually set the bedroom on fire and it was moving into the bathroom. I got out safely though. Thank God the bathroom had a window and I escaped that way. Too bad for my man Quentin. They say he was still in bed, shot three times, and his body was completely burned to a crisp. I was so devastated. My mind was lost, and all I could think about was them killers, Quentin, and even Sonya.

I knew about Sonya. She was the reason Quentin and me argued. I heard he was seeing her, but now I know why. Quentin needed a chick to be down with him. I wasn't that chick, never would be. Quentin knew, and he'd rather have me stay a good girl. He used Sonya for all she had, or could give him. I found out later on that Sonya was missing. I bet they came back the night of Quentin's funeral and killed her. No one knew where her body was, but they probably damaged it like they did Quentin's. I wanted out, to start my life over.

Chapter One

I sat in the airport waiting on Veronica. She had an extra room in her house so she was letting me stay with her in California. She also had two other roommates, Jessica and Trixsy. I met them at Ramon's funeral. He's my brother that died in a plane crash a couple years back. Veronica took it hard and moved to California with Trixsy and Jessica. They were cool girls, different, but cool.

Although Ramon and Veronica never married, I considered her my sister-in-law. She met Ramon seven years ago at my graduation. She graduated with me, but I never knew her until they hooked up. Veronica was always the wild type and she liked to be naked. She used to pose nude all the time until Ramon got tired of it. He hated hearing about her stripping on amateur night.

When Ramon passed away, she moved to California with them crazy girls and became a stripper. Veronica was proof that all strippers weren't hoes. Sex to her was serious, she wasn't into one-night stands. She had to be committed to that man to have sex with him, and she had only been with one man since Ramon passed away. She broke up with that guy and was now single. She liked it like that because she was more into her dancing. I swear she was in love with her own body.

Jessica was wild, too, but in a wilder way. She was total opposite of Veronica. Jessica loved sex and she'd have sex with any man, she was not picky at all. She was a very beautiful woman and got all kinds of attention, especially her 40DDs. They we're fake, but beautiful. She made me want to trade in my 36C's. Jessica loved to flaunt her breast and would show them off to anybody. The crazy thing about her was she was going to law school. I called her a professional slut. That's what she was, so there you go.

Trixsy was a gold digger. That girl never had one man, and she was into them rich men. She didn't care how they made their money, if they had it, they was her man. I admit, I wanted a man with money, too, but I also wanted love. She was like a female pimp. She didn't want love, ever. Trixsy didn't work, but drove a Benz and her hair and nails were always done. The girl got paid, and claimed she didn't have sex with those guys.

I didn't know coping with Quentin's death would be so hard. It didn't seem so bad when Ramon died. I bounced right back and went on with my life. I loved my brother, and I grieved for him, but I couldn't seem to stop grieving over Quentin. Right now, it feels as if I can never go on.

When I saw Veronica, I didn't get excited. She came over to me and hugged me, and we stood there forever, crying. When we got to the house she took me to my room and unpacked my things for me. All the girls helped me out. I couldn't have asked for more. That first week I stayed in the house and mostly slept in my bedroom.

I was left with $15,000, plus $20,000 that I found in the basement. There was also some dope that I gave to his brother. It wasn't worth much, but he gave me $10,000 for it as well as paid for the funeral to look out for me. Moving to California, I would have a change of life. My lifestyle wasn't bad, but I didn't want to deal with it anymore. I wanted a man with a real job, and I wanted my own job. I was going to be independent from now on. I gave them $5,000 and figured that would cover me until I could get on my feet. Veronica told me to take my time, but I knew I had to find me a job to pay my share of the rent. We lived in a big ass house and the mortgage was $2800 a month. The girls were happy a fourth woman moved in to split it four ways. The house had five bedrooms, and we each had our own with our own bathroom. The fifth bedroom was turned into a huge closet.

Those girls had so many clothes that they mixed and matched. Veronica, who was about a size ten, wore everyone's clothes. Out of all of us, she had the sexy curves and the big ass that every stripper wanted. Trixsy was the skinniest, wearing a five. She had curves but not like us. Her body was the average woman's body you would see in the magazine. Her whole appearance would trick you because she was a white woman, but when she opened her mouth, she sounded like Buckwild from *Flavor of Love*. Trixsy tanned so much she was almost my complexion, which was a beautiful honey bronze. She didn't care though, she was Trixsy. Me and Jessica both wore a size eight and we all had fly clothes.

It was 2:30 in the afternoon when I decided to get up. It had actually been two weeks since Quentin's death and I wasn't feeling any better, but staying up in the room wouldn't help. I walked out my room and started looking around the house. I had a tour, but never actually looked around. I peeked into each bedroom and was able to tell whose room was whose by their personality. Their rooms told it all. Soon as I was done exploring upstairs, I walked down the back stairway that led to the kitchen. There were two stairways. One leading to the front living room and the other leading to the kitchen.

Trixsy was at the stove cooking something. I definitely smelled a pie baking. I stood at the edge of the counter and waited for her to notice me. Soon as she saw me, she dropped the spoon and walked over to me. She embraced me with a hug and I hugged her back.

"You a'ight today?" she asked me.

"Yeah." I tried to smile.

Trixsy pulled me by the hand and brought me to a stool at the island table. "I'm cooking early today," she said. "Come sit down."

I sat at the table and Trixsy went back to the stove. I pulled my knees up to my chest and waited for Trixsy to bring my food. I watched her as she put a big steak on the plate along with some carrots and potatoes. Then, she pulled a bowl out the refrigerator and added the pasta salad on the plate. She sat it in front of me and then she sat across from me. I gave her a half smile.

"You haven't really ate anything," she said. "You'll feel better when you eat."

"My stomach is not ready for this yet."

"You been in that room for almost two weeks. You haven't eaten a good meal since."

"I ate."

"Yo' ass was nibbling on shit. You ain't eat a gotdamn thang!"

I laughed a little at Trixsy. She looked like the girl next door, all preppy and cute, but when she open her mouth it was full of filth, and she had a down south accent to go with it.

"What you laughin' fo'?" she asked me.

"Nothing." I picked up the fork. "You crazy, girl."

"That's what they say." She smiled with me.

I ate some of the carrots and it was pretty good, but Trixsy's face was all twisted up like I shouldn't be eating it. She just told me to eat, she didn't say what.

"You better eat that steak!"

"Okay, I will." I cut a small piece of the steak. "Quit rushing me." I took a small bite and I was pleased. It was so tender and juicy. A little spicy, but I liked it like that. "It's real good," I commented.

"I usually do most of the cooking, and I can cook my ass off."

"Now you have some competition, 'cause I can cook my ass off, too!"

Trixsy laughed. "That might be a good thang. Them other bitches can't cook worth a shit. They busy anyway. Jessica works and go to school. When she ain't doing that, she sleeping with somebody man." We both laughed. "Veronica usually go into work about 5:00, which is around dinner time. So, I'm left to cook and eat by myself."

"I didn't know Jessica had a job. I thought she was only going to school."

"She's a secretary at a law firm."

"That's good." I looked around. "Where's Veronica?"

"Shopping."

"All them clothes she got? She don't need to be shopping."

"Actually, she's looking for a TV for her bedroom. Hers went out."

"I had a few TVs. I kept everything in the house. It's up for sale, so whoever buys it don't need to furnish it." I paused. "Well, except for the bedroom. It was burned down. Everything else was okay."

"Girl, we could've used a little bit of everything."

"They still there if you guys want it."

"That's cool."

The phone rang and Trixsy got up to answer it. "Hello?" she sang. "Whas up?....Now?.....Well I cooked dinner, so I guess you can come through. Hold on a minute." She looked over at me. "You mind if my friend come through?"

"I don't care. I'm going back to my room anyway."

Trixsy put the phone back to her ear. "Tommie, you come over when you ready.....Okay....Bye."

Trixsy hung up the phone, and walked back to the table. She smiled as she sat down.

"You're not going back to your room." She was serious. "I want you to meet a good friend of mine."

"A good friend?" I questioned. "That sounds more like a boyfriend."

"Tommie is no boyfriend. He's just a friend that gives me money. He's the only one that gets special treatment."

"Special treatment?"

"We fuck."

I got quiet. She said that bluntly. "Oh. So why he get special treatment?"

"Wait till you see him, you'll see why. He so damn sexy and tall, and he has a smooth bald head that he rubs between my thighs."

"And he has money?"

"Damn right he has money. He a drug dealer."

"So why not just settle down with him?"

"We can't," she said. "He's a playa, and I love other men's pockets. I'm no hoe, Zaria. Tommie's the only one that get this pussy."

"So you don't care if he fucks other women?"

"All power to him." She grinned. "As long as he keeps my pockets fat, it's all good!"

I just looked at Trixsy. She was in love with money, and money only. She was what you would call a high class gold digger. She didn't play around. She got real money. Veronica told me when her guys give her money it ain't no hundreds. If she wanted her hair done, she'd get $1000, and her hair didn't cost that much. She had a lot of money that she just stacked. I guess she was saving it for a rainy day.

I was ready to get up and go. I really didn't feel like meeting Trixsy's friend, especially at a time like this. I was not strong enough.

"I'll take my plate to my room," I said, excusing myself from the table.

"Are you sure you don't want to meet Tommie?"

"I'll meet him another day. Sorry."

Trixsy gave me another hug. "It's all good."

"Thanks for dinner."

"I'll cook for you anytime."

"Okay, I'll remember that."

I walked back upstairs to my room, set the plate of food on my dresser, and curled up on my bed. Thinking of Trixsy and Tommie being together brought back memories of me and Quentin. At that moment, I cried until I feel asleep.

Chapter Two

I felt like I hadn't slept in days when really, all I had been doing was sleeping. There was a knock at my bedroom door along with a voice calling my name. I sat up in the bed and yelled come in. Veronica walked in, looking fly as ever, as if she was going out. It was Friday night, so she probably was going out. She looked around my room, then back at me.

"Have you noticed anything?" she asked me.

I looked at her, and then I looked around my room like she did. I was still sleepy and my room look the same since I been there.

"What?" I mumbled.

"I organized your clothes, shoes, purses, and put them in the walk in closet. I put all your under garments and pajamas in your dresser drawers."

How did she even know I wanted her to go through my stuff? I may not have even wanted my stuff in the same walk in, bedroom closet, or whatever the hell they called that bedroom. I wasn't going to trip though. She was only trying to help me and I figured I could deal with my clothes being in there.

"Thank you."

Veronica sat on my bed next to me. She ran her hand through my hair and smiled at me.

"Me and the girls planned something for you tonight." She then rubbed my face. "You're so pretty, you shouldn't be hiding in this house. We're taking you out."

"I'm not feeling all that well."

"Well, I guess not." She pointed to my plate of food from earlier. "You didn't even eat that steak."

"I'm not ready to leave this house."

Veronica stood up, and then she pulled me up, too. She put my arms around her neck, she was trying to pull me together. It worked a little until I broke down right in her arms. I started crying like a baby. Veronica just grabbed me harder, hugging me and brushing her hands through my hair.

"I know that feeling, Zaria, and you know I know. You got me through Ramon's death, and that was really hard for me. You seen how I was, but I had to pull it together. You told me that. Remember? You told me Ramon wants me to be strong for him. You said Ramon's going to be watching me and he don't want to see me like that. It would make him sad. Smile. God wants Quentin closer to him. He's better off, and God knew that."

"Do you think Quentin's in heaven?" I asked.

Veronica took a deep breath. She sat me down on my bed and sat next to me.

"Honey, Quentin sinned! Quentin sinned a lot, but Quentin never forgot about God. Even though Quentin was no saint, I believe he made it to paradise, just like Ramon. They don't mean to sin. Honey, Christians sin. Quentin being a drug dealer is no difference from Pastor Range taking God's money from the collection plate and spending it on them hoes. I gave him a private show once. Honestly, Pastor Range knows better. He s'pose to work for God. He worse than Quentin selling drugs."

Veronica brought a slight smile to my face. She told me about Pastor Range before, and he did know better. His sneaky ass.

"Everyone sins," Veronica continued. "So does that mean everyone goes to hell?"

"So who goes to hell?" I asked.

"In your heart right now, do you believe Jesus died on the cross for you?"

"Yeah."

"Good. As long as you believe that, then God will let you go to Paradise."

Veronica then stood up and pulled me up with her. "This is my belief," she said. "I strip, I drink, and I have sex before marriage. I don't do this shit on purpose, but I repent. I pay my tithes and everything. The whole world does what I do or worse. I'm going to Heaven to see my God."

I smiled. "Thank you. I feel better already."

"Now promise me to smile at Quentin's picture instead of crying over it, wishing he was here with you. He's okay. You're the one who's not. Me and you both, honey."

"Yeah, he's okay," I agreed and sighed. "Now where are you guys taking me?"

"Are you down for this?" she asked.

"For what?" She was scaring me. What did I get myself into?

"Wear something sexy."

"Where are we going?"

"It's a surprise."

I sighed and Veronica gave me one last hug. She did lift my spirits and I appreciated that in her. She always had a good heart. I decided I could let her and the girls take me out. It won't be so bad.

Chapter Three

I walked downstairs to the living room. The girls were sitting on the couch talking and laughing. I took a little longer getting ready but they didn't rush me. The room became quiet when they noticed me.

"Looks like I got real competition," Jessica joked.

"You look real good, girl," Veronica commented.

"I didn't know your hair could come back to life so quick," Trixsy said. "Earlier your hair was looking a hot mess!"

I just stood at the bottom of the staircase and smiled. I knew I was looking good. "Seems like I lost a little weight, but I still fit these shorts." I did a little spin so the girls could see me in my itty bitty shorts.

"Yo' ass ain't go nowhere!" Trixsy laughed along with the other girls.

My shorts were more than itty bitty. They were some coochie cutters. I was a hot dresser, those girls couldn't touch me, not even Veronica in her skintight Versace mini dress. Quentin made sure I had only the finest of everything. I bet Veronica was saying wow when she unpacked my clothes.

Jessica stood up and walked a circle around me. "You sure didn't lose no ass. Maybe your waist, but you got a nice ass. I'm jealous!"

"Thank you." I was embarrassed be cause they all were staring at me.

"I have a feeling me and you are going to be close," Jessica said, then walked away.

She was scaring me. Veronica didn't tell me Jessica was a lesbian. Maybe not. I was probably just being paranoid because she all up in my space. Besides, that girl was too much of a freak. She loved dick too much, and would fuck just about anybody. Maybe that *did* include women. Oh shit!

"So are my girls ready?" Veronica asked.

"Hell yeah we ready!" Jessica yelled.

"You got money?" Veronica asked me. "'Cause where we going, you need lots of money."

"I got enough."

All I had in my purse was two hundred dollar bills and a twenty, it better be enough. We rode in Veronica's black Denali. I had a black Escalade back at my mom's house. I told her to keep that for me until I come back for it. Right now, I had have no transportation.

I sat up front with Veronica. I was still miserable, but I tried hard not to show it because I didn't want to ruin our night. The girls were singing loud in the car. Veronica had the radio on with Beautiful Mind blasting from the system. That song *Ride* was playing.

"I'll ride his ass!" Veronica shouted over the music.

"Not before me, you won't!" Trixsy argued. "I'll put it on his fine ass. He won't know how to act. He'll be paying all my bills when I'm through with him."

"Whatever, bitch!" Jessica yelled out. "He ain't going no where after I'm through with him. I'm an expert when it comes to sex, so fuck all ya'll!"

Jessica was already drunk and still drinking. I couldn't believe I moved in with those crazy ass women.

It wasn't long before we pulled up at a club. As we walked toward the club, I noticed the line was full of females.

"Where all the guys?" I asked.

"Inside." Veronica smiled. I looked around the line again. "Butt ass naked!" Veronica finished the sentence.

"What?" I asked.

"Honey, we at the hottest male strip club ever known. The finest and sexiest men work here. Men up in here look like Beautiful Mind and LL Cool J."

"Yeah, and Imma find the one that look like Beautiful Mind!" Jessica said, dancing to the music we heard from the inside.

"I never been to a strip club before."

"First time for everything," Jessica said as she licked her glossy lips.

Now I was nervous. I didn't want to see naked ass men swinging their big ass dicks in my face. Okay, maybe. I needed something to take my mind off the tragedy.

The show was about to start any minute. Veronica had us sitting in the front row because she knew the owner and got us these wonderful seats. Lucky us! Jessica's freaky ass was all ready. She had a whole bunch of dollar bills in her hand. Now I wished I had broken those hundred dollar bills. I had to use my twenty to get in, and Veronica was buying my drinks all night. I guess no strippers would be getting a tip from me.

It was on when the first stripper came out. Chocolate Thug was his name. Damn, he looked good, too. He had long, black dreads and his dark chocolate body was full of muscle and bulk. The name fit his thuggish looking ass, too. My kind of man. I let all the other girls go wild for him, though. I wasn't the type of chick to be flippin' over guys like that.

The next two strippers didn't interest me. One stripper, Mr. Man, freaked the hell out of Jessica. They looked like they were having sex on stage. She was like a toy to him. He humped her, licked her tits, and had his head all between her legs. She hardly wore panties, so I knew he was surprised when he opened her legs and saw straight pussy! I think she was taking Mr. Man home.

I did enjoy myself, but I felt bad because I didn't have money to put down their boy thongs. I thought about getting up and breaking my bills. Every time I tried, a new guy came out. I didn't want to miss anything. I had to give them something. Soon as I got up, they called another stripper. His name was White Chocolate. I figured I could miss him, he a white boy anyway. I did a double take at that white boy and sat my happy ass back down. Damn! White Chocolate was the finest of them all. He was the only white man, and his ass was built to capacity. His ripped, tanned body was all oiled up. He had blond hair that was spiked up into a fade and he had ocean blue eyes that lit up the whole room. I was more than ready for him as I just sat there and watched. That man danced his ass off, too. I didn't mean to, but my pussy was wet over him. I was enjoying the moment.

White Chocolate noticed me looking at him lustfully. He had the nerve to dance over to my area and gave me a nice long dance. I was hot! He wasn't as nasty as Mr. Man, but up close he was fine and his body was hard. This white boy proved that white boys had big dicks, too. He had to be packing about ten inches. He was showing me that he wanted me as he danced on me like there were no other women around. I want him, too. It got so bad that I slipped both hundred dollar bills in his G-string. He never even paid attention. He stared into my eyes the whole time he did the nasty on me. Jessica even tried to steal White Chocolate from me, but he wasn't paying her any attention to her. Good! My heart dropped when it was time for him to exit the stage. That was one hot ass man. White Chocolate was last, so our fun was over. Jessica quickly got up and looked around.

"I got to find me some dick tonight!" she said.

"Yo' nasty ass." Trixsy called her out.

"Don't hate," she said, walking away.

"Whatever," Trixsy yelled to her.

We stood around the club for a while, socializing and drinking. I didn't know anyone, so I waited outside by the car. I just wanted the fresh air. I had to admit, I had lots of fun. Veronica brought it out of me. She really loved me as a sister-in-law and I loved her, too.

Those women were all over them strippers when they came outside. They were giving out autographs like they were celebrities. It seemed like the most famous one was White Chocolate. He had tons of females at his feet. I just watched and stared, and fantasized about his hot ass body in my bed. All the things he was doing to me in there, I imagined him doing it to me while we were naked. Oh shit! I was on fire. I snapped out of it when I saw him walking my way. I got nervous as hell. He had the most coolest walk and he looked so good in them Evisu jeans and that white t-shirt. I had never thought about being with a white man until now. I had never even looked twice at a white man, but he was sexy. Soon as he approached me, he grabbed my hand and kissed it. What a damn gentlemen. You couldn't find a man like that. But then again, his slick ass could be a player. He had women still flocking behind him.

He turned toward the women. "Excuse me, ladies, I need some privacy." Soon as they left he smiled at me. "How you doing?"

"I'm okay," I said calmly. "Just wondering why you'd leave all them women to come talk to me?"

"Why not?" he said. "You stand out. When I got on that stage you were all I saw."

"Oh yeah?"

"On the real, you is hot!"

"Are you sure it's not because I tipped you two hundred dollars?"

White chocolate smiled. "You gave me that?"

"So you didn't notice what I put in your g-string?" I flirted.

"I was noticing more of your beauty."

"Oh yeah?"

"The ladies you were with come regularly. Them some fine ass ladies, but you topped them all."

"Do you always hit on your customers?"

"Actually, no."

"So I'm the first?"

"I never dated my customers, I never slept with them, and I never have conversation with them. I always keep it short."

"Do you freak them like Mr. Man freaks the women?"

"Yeah." He smiled. "I can get down nastier than that."

"So why didn't you?"

"I wanted to, but you was already looking uncomfortable."

"Not me." I blushed.

I was more than embarrassed in front of this professional stripper, but I didn't want him to see that. The only other man that had been all over me like that was Quentin. He used to strip for me all the time.

I stood in front of White Chocolate feeling nervous and I wanted him to leave, only because he was too fine to be standing in front of me.

"Would you feel more comfortable if I took you out to dinner tomorrow night?" he asked me.

I hesitated and looked around. Not really. It was too soon for me to go out with another guy, Quentin would be pissed. Then, I thought about all the females he fucked every week. Especially Sonya. I guess it would be okay. It was just a harmless dinner date. Before I could answer him, I saw Veronica and Trixsy walking our way. They would give me so much trouble if I passed him up. Then again, they might steal him from me. Especially Jessica. Where was she at?

"Okay," I told White Chocolate.

He pulled out his cell phone and programmed my number. We set our date for 6:00 the next evening. Veronica and Trixsy finally arrived, but stayed back to give us privacy.

"These are my girlfriends, Veronica and Trixsy," I said, pointing them out so they would come closer. "Jessica is somewhere around." I spoke too soon because she came quick. It was like she knew we were with White Chocolate and her antennas went up. "That's Jessica," I told him as she arrived.

"Nice to meet all you ladies." He smiled at them.

"Are you free tonight?" Jessica asked as she stepped all in his face.

He looked at me and gave me a strange look. *Yeah, she a hoe! I know already,* was what I was thinking.

He stared at Jessica from the bottom up. He stared at every asset of her body. For a moment, I thought he was thinking about it. He seemed to like the way her tits were popping out. She wanted him bad, and I could tell. Her slut ass didn't know he asked me out already. It shocked me when White Chocolate turned toward me, grabbed my hand, and kissed it again. I watched Jessica's face and saw jealousy in it. She looked like she wanted to kill me. I was glad he totally ignored her fake ass.

"I'll be calling you," he said to me.

"I'll be waiting." I blushed.

He looked at my girls again. "Alright then, ladies. Thanks for coming to the show."

We all watched his fine ass walk away. Soon as he hit a distance where he couldn't hear us, the girls went crazy.

"You gave White Chocolate your phone number?" Veronica asked me.

"He asked," I told her.

"He asked for your number?" Jessica was hating.

"Why not?" I twirled around. "I look good!"

"Well, you make sure you keep that hot ass white boy!" Trixsy said. "Hold on tight!"

"We're only going out as friends."

"Good," Jessica stepped in, "when you done with dinner, bring his ass home and I'll fuck him good!"

"No the fuck you won't!" I started to get mad at

her hoeish ass.

"You seen how he looked at me. He wants me."

"He looked at them fake tities."

"It's okay, honey," Jessica licked her lips, "we can have a threesome,. I'm not stingy."

Damn that Jessica! I was not going to like her. I could see that now. White Chocolate didn't want her. He was hotter than hot, too hot for Jessica. Her ass for damn sure would not steal him away from me.

****

That night I went to sleep without crying my eyes out. I talked with Quentin for a while, and apologized to him if he thought I was moving too fast. I still loved him and I would never forget Quentin. If he wanted me to be happy, he'd understand. I smiled as I closed my eyes, awaiting the next night to be with White Chocolate.

Chapter Four

It was 8:20 in the morning when the phone rang. I let it ring, hoping one of the other girls would pick it up. After about five rings, I heard the answering machine come on. It was in the hallway between our bedrooms. Jessica's hot ass was the one that recorded the greeting.

"You've reached the sexy household of Jessica, Veronica, Trixsy, and Azaria. I know you're disappointed that no one is home, but please leave a message, and we'll get right back at cha'. Have a wonderful day!"

There was a long pause after that recording, then a deep, sexy voice came on.

"Good morning, beautiful women." It was White Chocolate.

Soon as I heard his voice, I rushed out into the hallway to try and stop the recording. When I entered the hallway, Jessica popped her head out her room, then Trixsy, then Veronica. I didn't stop the recording, I decided to let them listen. He might say something sweet about me.

"Sorry to call so early," he stated. "I just wanted to say good morning to Azaria, and I wanted you to come jogging with me. It would be nice to have a partner this morning."

Before he could finish, I picked up the phone.

"Hello?"

"So you're up?" He sounded like he was smiling.

"I was up."

"Good. I jog every morning and I was hoping you come join me."

"Sure."

"Cool. Can I pick you up?"

"Yeah."

"You'll be ready in thirty minutes?"

"Yeah."

"So where do you live?"

I looked at Veronica, who was smiling at me hard. I guess she was happy for me. I had lived there for about two weeks, and didn't know the address. I whispered to her, asking for the address.

"202 Florist Lane," she told me.

I mouthed thank you to her and she smiled back.

"Azaria?" White Chocolate called my name. "You still there?"

"Sorry. It's 202 Florist Lane."

"Okay, ma. Be ready.!"

"I will."

I hung up the phone and looked at all the girls. They all seem so excited, even Jessica, *the hater!* Jessica stepped out her room. "Girl, I may joke around with you sometimes, but I'm honestly happy to see you happy. Even if it is with a man I want to fuck. So you better not fuck it up."

"He just want me to go running with him. I wouldn't get into a relationship now."

"It may take some time, but he better be there when you're ready."

I walked away laughing. I was more happy that I had friends. I never had any friends when I was with

Quentin. All the females in New York hated me 'cause I had him. I was envied and hated by many, just because I had the sexiest man in New York. Finally, I felt important and loved by some women. I really needed it at the time, and I was so thankful.

I took a quick shower and put on my sexiest sweat suit. It was white Baby Phat velour shorts, with a pink sports bra under the velour jacket. The jacket showed my belly, so I put my pink diamond belly ring in. I brushed my hair into a high ponytail so it could shake when I ran. By the time I slipped on my white Air Max, the doorbell rang. It was Jessica that answered the door. I watched her from the top step as she was flirting.

"Do you have any brothers?" she asked him.

"I have two," he responded while looking around the house. "One's older and one's younger."

"Do they look anything like you?"

I watched White Chocolate shake his head at her. I knew he was thinking, *hurry up, Azaria.* He probably thought she was crazy, but he was pretty nice about it and answered her question.

"We all look alike," he answered.

"You let the older one know I said what's up." She winked.

"I'll be sure to do that." I made my presence be known and walked downstairs. Jessica looked my way, and stepped back from White Chocolate. "Oh, I see you're ready. And looking good," I heard White Chocolate mumble.

Soon as I reached the bottom step, he took a step toward me and kissed my hand. I loved the treatment he gave me.

"You work out often?" he asked me.

"I used to run a lot, actually."

He walked around me, admiring my toned body. "I can see that you run a lot."

"I hope you two have a good time," Jessica interrupted.

"Thanks, Jessica," I said told her.

"Don't forget about me, Mr. White Chocolate," Jessica said before she walked away.

"Tony," he corrected her.

"Well, see you later, Tony."

So that's his name, Tony. Well, Tony sure was a White Chocolate, and a gentlemen at that. We walked outside and I saw his shiny black F-150, four door. It was hot with the chrome rims on it. He drove a big truck. I wasn't complaining because I liked a man who drove a big truck.

Tony opened the passenger door for me and I slipped in. It was nice and comfortable inside. They say you can tell about a man from the inside of his car. His car looked like it was fresh from the lot with the new car smell. He had a nice deck that looked custom made. The stereo system was fresh as hell. The car was clean with nothing in it but a bottle of Aquafina in the cup holder. I say he got money. I could imagine what his house looked like.

Tony just drove around for a while and we got to know each other more. I loved his personality. He was real cool and so down to earth. He dressed like a thug, but he didn't act like what society would call "black". He was just Tony. He even grew up on a farm. I never expected that because he was so hip.

"So how'd you meet your room mates?" he asked. "I never seen you with them before."

"I'm from New York."

"I shoulda known. You got the accent. So what brings you here? Cali's a far way from home."

"Veronica is like my sister-in-law," I told him. "She dated my brother."

I took a long pause and it was like Tony sensed something was wrong. "Are you alright?" he asked.

"I'm fine. I just miss my family back at home."

I didn't want to tell him about Quentin because I hated the sympathy. I knew he would probably hug me and treat me different. Besides that, I didn't know Tony all that well.

"What made you want to move to Cali?"

"Veronica needed me, and I needed her. I wanted a new environment. I guess it was time to start a new life."

Tony paused. "If you don't mind me asking, why are you trying to leave that part of your life?"

"Who said I was? I just wanted to move here."

He smiled. "You're very hesitant, so I figured something was wrong."

"Nothing bad. I heard you guys know how to get down here, so I moved here."

"Yeah, we can get down."

I stayed quiet for awhile, hoping not to go back to that subject. I started talking before I broke down and told him I lost my boyfriend and some people were after me.

"I don't want to make this comment to be racist, but you're no ordinary white boy. You damn sure don't dance like one."

Tony laughed it off. I couldn't tell if he didn't mind the question or what. His whole body language changed. He shifted more toward the door and glanced over at me. He didn't frown, which was a good sign. Instead, he smiled, showing off two dimples and white teeth. Damn he fine!

"My parents claim they weren't racist, but they hate to be around black people," he admitted.

"Are you serious?"

I was shocked because the way Tony acted, you would think he was raised by a black family.

"It didn't rub off on me or my brother, Allen, who's the youngest. Allen had two children by a black woman. My older brother, Mark, is married to a white woman. He's not racist though. He's cool, too."

"So how did you and Allen start loving black women if your parents tried to keep you away from them?"

"Me and Allen are close in age, we went to school together. We were more curious than ever when we got to school and saw the opposite of what our parents were teaching us. My dad would say black people are lazy and never wanted to do nothing with themselves. I go to school and see Marcus Greene, who was the captain of the football team, and had better grades than me. Dante Miller was captain of the basketball team. It seem like majority of the popular kids were black." Tony smiled. "Then, for some reason, I was loving the sistahs. Tonya Jones broke my virginity. After that episode I didn't want a white woman, even though I did date a couple. But, I was more loving black women. I love ass, and ya'll got plenty of it."

I laughed. "Did you love them white women you dated?"

"No. I only dated two, and it was for a very short time. I couldn't do it."

"Why?"

"I love a black woman's attitude. Not that ghetto ass type, I can't deal with that. I love everything about a black woman. I love her skin, lips, nice ass....I love black women!"

"Do I fit what you love?"

"Honestly, you're the finest woman I have ever met. You're gorgeous.!" I blushed for a moment and looked down. He brushed the back of his hand across my face. "I would love to make you my woman," he said.

I was speechless. Tony was making me feel good. "Was that a statement?" I asked.

"It was more of a question." He licked his lips.

"What do you know about me?"

"Well, you're a beautiful woman who needs a good man like me."

"I don't need a man."

"Maybe not, but you at least need a friend."

I laughed. "And let me guess, you'll be that friend?"

"That's right." He smiled.

"Okay, you're my new friend."

"So, can I take my new friend somewhere?"

"I thought we were going jogging."

"We were, up until I seen how hot you look. You can't be running looking all sexy. I won't be able to focus. I just want to look at you all day anyway."

I made this man fall in love. Damn! So now what? I bet he wanted to take me to his house. He was still a total stranger to me. I was a fool when it came to men. I fell in love too quick.

"Take me to your house," I demanded.

He looked over at me. "Seriously?"

"Yeah, I want to see where you live."

"Okay."

Tony made a quick u-turn and headed to his house. I was only wanting to chill for awhile. That's all. Straight up!

Chapter Five

6:30 that evening, I was sitting on Tony's sofa laughing my ass off. I spent all day at his house, just forgetting about my past. Tony cooked me breakfast, lunch, and had started dinner. All we did was talk. We tried to watch a couple of movies, but we talked all through them. I felt like I knew Tony so well. It seemed like he'd been my friend forever. He even told me about personal things, like his sex life. Me on the other hand, didn't tell him personal business, like Quentin. I didn't forget Quentin, and Lord knows I never will. It was just hard for me to talk about him. I could tell Tony was going to be a good friend to talk to.

I knew the girls were probably worried about me since I didn't have a cell phone that they could blow up. Knowing them crazy girls, they might have thought Tony kidnapped me, so I excused myself to use Tony's house phone. I took the cordless phone into the bathroom with me and I was mad when I heard Jessica's voice on the other end.

"What up, girl?" I said to her.

"Azaria!" she screamed into the phone.

"Sorry, I lost track of time."

"I thought you ran off with Mr. White Chocolate."

"He cooked for me," I explained. "Then we talked all day and I forgot about ya'll."

"Did you fuck him?" she blurted out.

"No! He's just a friend, and friends don't fuck."

"Whatever," she said as if she didn't believe me. "I'll let the girls know you're okay. We were over here worried about you."

"Well thank you. Tony will drop me off later."

"Take your time. Make his white, sexy ass show you that big dick again. It's a monster and I would love for him to stick it in me. I know he got black in him. Do he?"

I laughed. "Bye, Jessica."

I hung up the phone and smiled to myself. She's cool, but her ass was so nasty. I was sitting on the seat of the toilet and could hardly get up. Tony fed me too much food. I drank a lot of wine, too. Maybe he put something in my drink. I shouldn't think like that, but it's possible. He didn't look like that type of person to drug women and take advantage of them. Looks could be deceiving though.

I walked out the bathroom and back into the living room. Tony was in the kitchen cleaning up. He was a very clean man, a little too clean. He noticed me in the living room and came in drying his hands.

"You let me know when your ready to go home," he told me.

"Are you trying to kick me out?"

"Baby, you can stay all night long. I love your company."

"Good, 'cause I like your company, too."

Tony walked over to me and sat down on the couch, pulling me next to him. I was nervous, so I inched away from him. He had to put something in my wine because it was making me horny. Maybe it was just me sitting next to a stripper. I knew I couldn't let myself get too close to Tony because Quentin was still my boyfriend, dead or alive. The ten years we had been together, not once had I cheated on him. Come to think about it, it was my first opportunity with another man, but not this soon. Quentin would be turning in his grave.

Tony kept staring at me and whispering sweet nothings in my ear. I just giggled 'cause it tickled. His whispering was making my panties more than wet. Tony knew what he was doing. Right then, I became curious about this white boy. I did want to fuck him, and I wanted him right now!

"Let me ask you something," I flirted.

"What's that?"

"Do white guys like to…you know?"

"What?"

I played dumb. "You know?"

"Eat pussy?" He licked his lips.

"Yeah."

Tony licked his lips again. "I love eating pussy."

I giggled. "Why is that? They say it's because white guys got little dicks, but after seeing what you was packing, that's a myth."

"Baby, it don't matter the color of your skin. Big dicks can be on anyone. Little dicks can be on anyone. Size don't matter." He moved in closer to me and started kissing my neck. "I get a kick out of licking pussy. I love how it tastes. I love to hear you call my name. I love to see you squirm and ask for more."

"I can yell your name and squirm around without you licking my pussy. Would you like that?"

"I'd love that, too, but I want to make you go wild."

"You think I'll go wild?"

Tony started rubbing on my thigh. "You'll be

climbing the walls."

"You think so?" I flirted back.

"Yelp." He was now licking all in my ear and on my neck.

Damn! His sexy voice made it very tempting. He had his hand all the way between my thighs and I bet he could feel my wetness through my shorts. What the hell, I gave in. I turned toward him and we kissed passionately. His hands then found their way inside my shorts and into my panties. I opened my legs wider, and let his fingers go to work. The more passionate our kiss got, the deeper his three to four fingers got. Tony didn't play around when it came to finger fucking. Soon as my juices flowed all over his fingers, he licked them clean. Tony didn't waste no time pulling off my shoes and my shorts. He had me on the edge of the sofa and his face between my legs. I swear he put a love spell on me the moment his tongue touched my clit. No man, I mean no man, not even Quentin, could lick pussy that good. He was so good that when I saw him come up, I swear he was still down there sucking on my clit.

Next thing I knew, he was pulling off his clothes quick, and he flipped my ass over on my stomach. He was ready for doggy style. Tony worked the shit out of me, too. He pulled off my shirt and bra, and was still fucking me hard from the back. I didn't want him to stop, but a knock at the door interrupted our moment and caused him to stop for a quick second. That was only for a quick second. He started back up, trying to finish it off. He went faster and faster like a jackrabbit. The knock at the door got louder and louder. The person behind the door seemed mad as hell. Soon as Tony came, I was up. He came inside me with no condom on but I didn't care. I wanted to know who was at the door.

"Who is that?" I asked, pulling my shorts on.

Tony started shaking his head. "I'm sorry about this, baby."

"About what?"

"Tisha."

"Who's Tisha?"

"The woman knocking. She's my ex-girlfriend and she's a stalker. She won't leave me alone."

I grabbed my stuff and walked toward the back. "Get rid of her!"

I walked behind the wall in the next room where I could listen. I peeked around the corner to watch who came in. Tony put on his pants and opened the door. A tall, dark skinned woman entered and looked around. She seemed heated.

"I heard you fucking some bitch!" she yelled.

"What's wrong with you!" He grabbed her by the neck. "Leave me the fuck alone, nobody told your ass to come over here!"

He let her go and walked away from her. She held her neck and continued looking around.

"Where is she?" she asked.

"Don't worry about her." Tony grabbed Tisha by the arm and drug her to the door. "Get the fuck out my house!"

"Not until I see who's fucking my man." She pulled away from him.

"Leave, Tish!"

That's when I walked in. She stopped struggling and put her hands on her hips.

"Is that the bitch I heard you fucking?" She rolled her eyes at me.

I just stood there and smiled at her. That only made her madder. She looked back and forth from me to Tony. She moved Tony out the way and walked toward me. I walked toward her, too, I wasn't scared! I whooped plenty of bitches asses back in NY. Tony stepped in front of her. Lucky for her.

"Get out," he yelled to her.

"Do you know why he wants me to get out?" she asked me. "'Cause he don't want you to know."

"Know what?" I looked at Tony.

"I fucked him last night, okay! He told me to come back tonight. I don't know why you're here, Tony is only good to fuck. He's a liar and he's a dog!"

I looked over at Tony. All he could do was grab Tisha again.

"You fuckin' liar!" He pushed her away. "You lie too much!"

"So we didn't fuck last night?"

"I was alone," he yelled. "Azaria knows I worked last night. I did a show and she was there!"

"It was after the show," Tisha exclaimed. "Why you want to lie on me. We're engaged."

Tisha held up her hand, showing me her ring. I was so hot, I knew it was too good to be true.

"What's going on, Tony?" I asked him.

"Azaria, me and Tisha been broke up for six months. She don't think it's over."

"Did you guys have sex last night?"

"Baby, I swear we didn't. She did come by, but I made her leave right away. I don't want her. I want you."

"If you believe him, then your ass is stupid," she interrupted. "He cheated on me over twenty times."

"Get your lying ass out my house!"

"What about the ring?" I asked him.

"I proposed to her a year ago. She won't give me back my ring, so I let her keep it." Tony was sounding so sincere. "It's over between me and her."

"Why are you lying on me?" She began to cry. "I love you, Tony, and you do this to me?"

I grabbed my jacket and walked toward the door. Tony tried to grab me, but I pulled away from him. He kept trying to explain his side. I couldn't get involved with a man that had a girlfriend, or drama. I didn't want to have to hurt that bitch, because I would.

Tony got in front of me and tried to keep me from going out the door. His strong arms held onto me tight. I couldn't get out of his hold if I wanted to.

"Let me go!" I yelled. "I'll scream if you don't let me go!" He finally let me go and I turned toward him. "You should've told me about her," I yelled to him.

"What's there to tell? She's my ex, I don't want her!"

"Don't call me." I finally walked out his house.

I stood outside in Tony's yard, thinking about walking. I didn't even know where I was. I looked up at Tisha, who was now standing out on the porch. She had her arms folded across her chest with a little smirk on her face.

"Sorry," I yelled to her. "I didn't know he had a girlfriend."

Tony pushed her off his porch. "Get the fuck off my property!"

Maybe she wasn't his girlfriend, but I still didn't want to deal with that crazy girl. I started walking to nowhere because I had no idea where I was going. Tony ran behind me, still apologizing and explaining.

"Please, Azaria, believe me," he begged.

"I want to," I told him. "I just had sex with you. I didn't want no one-night stand. I'm not like that, but that bitch needs to go! If she keeps popping up, then I can't be with you. Just let me have time to think."

"Fine. Let me at least take you home."

I sighed and looked around the neighborhood. I had no choice, unless I called a cab or one of the girls.

"Just let me use your phone," I told him.

"I'll take you. You can even drive my truck home. I just want you to believe me. I wouldn't play you like that."

"Just let me use your phone."

Tony finally gave in and he went and got his cell phone. I called Jessica and gave her the address. Tony waited outside with me and I wished he wouldn't. He kept apologizing, pleading, and begging for me to believe him. I honestly wanted to believe him, but the whole time he was talking with me, that little tramp worked her way back in the house. She stood in the window with her bra and panties on. Tony didn't know and I wasn't going to tell him. He'd probably go in there and fuck her, too. He's a man.

Soon as Jessica pulled up, I hoped in the car quick. Tony grabbed my arm as I got in the car, and I gave him a look that made him let go so I could shut the door. Jessica pulled off right after that. It was just getting good, and now this!

Chapter Six

After telling the girls what happened, I went straight upstairs to my bedroom. They all thought I should give him another chance, but I was confused. I was mad at myself for giving my body to that man and trusting him. What the hell was I thinking?

While I was lying in the bed, I felt so sick to my stomach. I don't know what was wrong with me. Every time I got sad and depressed, my stomach started hurting and I felt sick. I had to stop doing this to myself. I ran into my bathroom because I felt I had to throw up. Soon as I flushed the toilet from throwing up, the girls walked into my room. I sat back on my bed and looked at all of them.

"What?" I asked, feeling dizzy. "I told ya'll I was tired."

"We just thought of something," Veronica said.

"Yeah?"

"Maybe you're pregnant."

"Yeah, by Quentin," Jessica explained.

Trixsy sat next to me on the bed. "You been sick since you came to the house. You're showing signs of pregnancy."

"No," I cried out. "I don't want to be pregnant."

"I have tons of pregnancy tests." Jessica walked toward the door. "I'm always hoping to be pregnant, but I can't get pregnant." She walked out the room and came back with a test and handed it to me. I stared at it, then slowly got up. "It'll detect whether you're pregnant or not," Jessica said. "It's early response."

"Well, pray that I'm not."

I walked into the bathroom and closed the door behind me. Good thing I held my pee from when I was at Tony's house. I sat on the toilet, I held the stick under me, and my pee flowed out. Soon as I was done, I took a quick peek, and then sat it down on the bathroom sink. It was still blank. Thank God. Next thing you know, there was a knock at the door.

"What does it say?" Veronica asked.

I opened the door. "I'm not looking."

I went back into my room and sat on the bed. Veronica went into the bathroom, picked it up, and then looked at me crazy.

"Is she pregnant?" Jessica asked.

Veronica smiled. "You're pregnant."

"No," I yelled. "Me and Quentin were always trying. Why now?"

"You have a part of Quentin with you," Trixsy added.

"I can't do this without Quentin."

"You have us," Veronica said.

"Thanks, but my baby needs a father figure, not four women. When I have a baby, he'll have a father."

"You're not getting an abortion," Veronica quickly said.

"I have to." I am not raising a child without his father. No man gonna want me if I have another man's baby anyway."

"Tony will take you no matter what," Jessica said.

"Tony is a liar," I cried.

"How do you know he's a liar? You never gave him a chance."

"I don't want to get hurt."

"Girl, you are a very lucky woman." Jessica hugged me. "Give that man a chance."

I became more and more devastated. I was pregnant and Tony had a girlfriend. I had sex with another woman's man. How sick was that? My mind went blank while the girls talked amongst each other. I just lay there in the bed looking lost. Shit, I was lost. I could even hear them girls planning my baby shower already. I didn't want this baby, not now.

Chapter Seven

A whole week rolled by and I was back into my depressed stage. My mom sent my truck so I had some transportation, but I wasn't going anywhere. I think Jessica's been joyriding in it, but I didn't care. I just locked myself in my bedroom. Tony was calling everyday and Veronica said he stopped by, too, but she always told him I was sleep. That was good because I was not into hearing him explain anymore about that Tisha bitch.

Friday rolled around again, and I was hearing a lot of commotion outside my door. I got up from my bed and cracked open the door. I heard music and a lot of people. I opened the door all the way and walked to the balcony of the stairs. The house was full to capacity of people. Were they having a party and didn't invite me? I quickly ran back to my room and shut the door. I looked a hot ass mess, and didn't want anybody to see me that way. I stood behind the door wondering what they were having a party for. Knowing them, they probably were partying to be partying. They should have woke me up and let me know. I was depressed, but I loved to party.

I ran to the big room where all the clothes were. I grabbed something cute and sexy, and ran back to my room. I went into my bathroom and took a shower as well as wash my hair, which took forever because it's so damn kinky and thick. Soon as I was done, I wrapped a towel around my body and my hair.

When I opened the door, I jumped a little because I was startled by a tall, black guy. He had his back toward me talking on a cell phone. He must've heard me gasp, because he turned around. Whoever he was talking to, he let them go and shut his phone. He smiled at me. He was the one blushing, as if he was embarrassed.

"I'm sorry, ma'am." He had a cute smile. "I thought everyone was downstairs. I just needed a little privacy. I'm truly sorry."

"It's okay." He was about to exit my bedroom. "Excuse me?" I asked.

He turned around like he was expecting that. "What's up?"

"Are they having a party?" I asked.

"You didn't know?"

"I've been kind of sick, and I isolated myself from everyone."

"So you live here in this house, too?"

"Yes."

He extended his hand out. "Sorry for not introducing myself. My name is Caddy."

"Caddy?" I repeated.

"Calvin is my birth name."

"Oh, so why Caddy?"

"'Cause all I drive is Caddy's. What you think?"

I laughed a little. "I was thinking that, but then I thought that was too simple."

"My brother gave me that name. My first car was a caddy, and I been driving one every since."

"Oh."

I stood there trying to hold my towel up. Caddy

leaned against my wall, eying me down. He reminded me of Quentin. Same complexion, same build, same eyes, and even the same smile. It was kinda scary.

"I guess I should get going," Caddy spoke.

"You're going out to that party?"

"Yeah."

"It'll only take me a moment to get dressed. You don't mind escorting me, do you?"

He smiled. "It'll be my pleasure."

"Have a seat, and I'll be out real quick."

I grabbed my outfit I picked out earlier and rambled around, looking for my bra and panties. I looked over at Caddy and I knew he was watching my every move, but he played it off like he was playing with his cell phone. I bent down in my bottom drawer to pick out a pair of thongs and when I stood up, I became nervous and dropped my towel.

"I'm not looking." He quickly turned his head.

I picked up my towel and gathered my things. "I'll be ready in a second."

I ran into the bathroom, lotioned up my body, and dressed. I forgot about the towel around my head. My hair was a good awful mess. I pulled the towel off, moused my hair, and wore my natural, wavy hair hanging down. I quickly pulled out my hair dryer and dried it, threw on a head band, and put on a little make-up. I was looking good in my quickest time getting ready. I opened the door and that fine man was on my bed, fast asleep. I looked at the clock and realized I was in there for more than thirty minutes. It didn't seem that long. Oh well, I wouldn't wake him. He might have been drunk anyway. I slipped on my sandals and quietly left my room.

It was so live downstairs. I stood at the top step

looking around, hoping to see one of the girls. The first one I spotted was Jessica, who seemed to be down someone's throat. The man was feeling all on her booty while they kissed. Next! I looked around for the other two. I saw Trixsy telling some bitch off. I mean, it looked like she was she letting the girl have it. I wondered what happened over there. I looked around for Veronica but couldn't find her. That was a good sign. I needed a drink, and she'd go crazy if she saw me with a drink.

I walked down the hall to the back stairs that led to the kitchen. I peeked in there and saw a whole bunch of strangers. I walked in and poured myself a rum and Coke. I stood there and drank away. I think I had three cups, and I was feeling mighty tipsy. One guy danced with me in the kitchen. We were dirty dancing, and I was shaking my ass all up on him. Other guys tried throwing game at me while I danced with him, but I didn't move because where we danced at, was where the drinks were at. I needed this, pregnant or not.

I just about passed out when I asked some guy to give me what he was drinking, and whatever it was tore me up. My night was blown when Veronica found me. Next to her was a fine man.

"Azaria!" she yelled out. "You're drunk! I didn't even know you were down here!"

"Can I kiss you?" I asked her date. He was fine.

"No," she yelled at me. "He's my date, and you need to go back and rest."

"I can't. I want to have fun."

Veronica helped me up. "You're way too drunk to be down here, and you're pregnant!"

I pulled away from Veronica, and then kissed her

on the cheek."Fine," I said. "I'll take myself to bed. Are you happy?"

"I'll walk you."

Veronica guided me upstairs. I fell at my bedroom door and I sat there for a minute.

"Okay, Veronica, I'm fine." I smiled at her. "Now go fuck that man, you need to."

Veronica laughed. "You are drunk. Let's get you into the bed."

"Let me hear the music for awhile."

"No, get up," she demanded.

"Come on, Veronica," I heard the man say. "She wants to chill out here. We'll check on her later."

Veronica looked at me. "Okay, I'll be back."

I watched her leave with her new friend then I slowly opened my door and crawled in. Once inside, I closed my door and locked it behind me so Veronica would leave me alone. I fell on top of my bed. That alcohol really did me in.

Chapter Eight

I had the most terrible headache when I woke up. I was hot and sweaty, and also butt naked. My mind was blank and I needed a cup of coffee. I slowly rose up and my hand touched an arm, a big, strong arm. I pulled the sheets back and saw a muscular, tattooed body on my bed. He was naked, too. I think it was that Caddy guy. What the hell did I do?"

"Caddy." I was shaking him. "Caddy!"

"What, baby?" he said, still asleep.

Caddy rolled over and smiled at me. He then tried kissing me, but I pushed him away.

"Did we fuck?" I yelled.

"Yeah."

"Oh shit." I pounded my fist in my bed.

"You started it by kissing on me. I tried pushing you away, but you started giving me head. I couldn't stop you then."

I looked down at his thang. "I gave you head?"

"Good head, too." He smiled.

"I had too much to drink," I cried.

"So you don't remember?"

"No, what happened?" I looked around my room, searching the dressers and the floors.

"What are you looking for?" he asked me.

"We didn't use a condom?"

"No, we didn't have one."

I screamed. "No!"

Caddy got up and searched around for his clothes. I was pissed, but I still noticed he did have a sexy ass. How could I be so drunk to and sleep with a stranger with no condom? Caddy quickly put on all his clothes wrote something on a piece of paper and handed it to me.

"That's my cell phone number. Call me when you want to fuck me sober."

I couldn't believe he had the nerve to say that. That nasty ass punk. Awww! I hated myself today. Not even thirty seconds after Caddy left, Jessica ran in my room. She looked surprised when she saw me naked. I pulled the sheet over my body.

"Where did he come from?" she asked.

"I was drunk and I slept with him." I continued to cry.

"Me and Trixsy heard you guys. We wanted to know who the fuck was Caddy. He was hittin' it hard, girl. All night you was calling Caddy. I wish I was the fly on the wall."

"I don't even remember sleeping with him."

Jessica walked in and closed the door behind her. She sat on the floor. "A lot of shit might be on that bed, 'cause ya'll was fucking all night. You use a condom?" I was silent. "You didn't," Jessica yelled. "You better hope the baby is alright. He might've punctured the wound."

"Honestly, I don't even care."

"Why?" She got serious. "I would love to have a baby."

"Quentin is dead! Who's going to help me?"

"Me, Veronica, and Trixsy will, too."

"You don't understand. I want my baby to have a father. I grew up with all women in the household and

I never had one. I couldn't go to the father/daughter dance in high school. I know what it's like not to have a father, and I don't want that for my child."

Jessica sat there silent, as if she was thinking. I think she knew what I was talking about. I was not going to raise a baby a single mother, without a father. That's not the life I dreamed about. I didn't even care if I wasn't married to my child's father. I just want to raise my baby with their father. Every child deserved one.

"I feel you." Jessica then started to smile. "But you're keeping the baby."

"No," I told her.

"You said Caddy didn't use a condom, right?"

I rolled my eyes. "No, we didn't."

"Good." She was excited.

"Good?" I was now confused.

"It's Caddy's baby."

I looked at Jessica like she was crazy. What the hell she thinking? That was the most craziest idea I had ever heard. But then again, Caddy did kind of favor Quentin. Maybe Caddy would think the baby was his. Then, he'd step up and help me take care of it. I mean, I didn't want any relations with him. I'd just let the man be my baby's daddy.

"I guess that's not a bad idea." I gave Jessica five.

"All you have to do is keep seeing him," Jessica instructed. "Then maybe after two or three weeks, surprise him with the news."

I slowly pulled the sheet away from me and got up. "Not a bad idea."

"So you're keeping the baby?

I looked at my naked body in the mirror. I poked my belly out, trying to imagine myself big. I didn't care that Jessica was in my bedroom. We were both women.

"Okay," I said, rubbing my belly. "I'll do it."

Jessica got up and threw her arms around me. We hugged, jumping up and down.

That's when Trixsy walked in and yelled, "Eeeewww! Ya'll nasty!"

I quickly let go of Jessica. I guess we got a little too happy. I grabbed my bathrobe and put it on.

"We're just happy," I said.

"So, you guys had sex or something?" Trixsy asked.

I rolled my eyes at that thought. "I just happen to be naked when she came into my room. We were talking about what I was going to do about the baby. I decided to keep it."

"Well I'm glad to hear that." Trixsy then showed me her love by also giving me a hug. At least this time I had a bathrobe on. "What made you change your mind?"

I looked over at Jessica. "Caddy."

Trixsy started to laugh. "Oh yeah, we heard you in here calling some guy name Caddy. What was that all about? Was his dick that big?"

"Honestly, I don't know. I was drunk."

"So who is this Caddy dude?" Trixsy asked, walking around my room. "Did he tell you he'd help you take care of your baby?"

"He don't know I'm pregnant."

Trixsy stopped walking and looked at me. "He don't know? Then why is he the reason you're keeping the baby?"

I looked back over at Jessica. She looked away as if it was all my idea. Now she didn't want to be behind me. So! I liked the idea and I was sticking to it.

"I'm going to tell him he got me pregnant," I revealed to Trixsy.

Trixsy's mouth dropped open. "You're going to do what!"

"You heard me right."

"Azaria, what made you think of something so stupid?"

"Jessica."

Jessica put her hands on her hips. "Admit it, Trixsy. That's a slick idea, huh?"

Trixsy hesitated. "Fuck it, Azaria. Get his money."

"Don't he favor Quentin? Did you see him when he left?"

"Yeah, I seen him," Jessica said. I knew she saw him, she just had to put her two cents in. "Ooohh, he's so damn good looking," she finished.

"Veronica might not like that idea," Trixsy said. Then she looked as if to wave it off. "Who cares what her boring ass say? I agree with Jessica."

Trixsy was right. Later on we told Veronica and she was pissed. She tried talking me out of it, but my mind was made up. Caddy was going to be my baby's daddy. I guess Veronica just had to go along with me. She was more than happy I was keeping the baby anyway.

Chapter Nine

Later on that night, I dialed Caddy's number. I had to start somewhere with him.

"I'm glad you called," he told me soon as he heard my voice.

"I thought you might've forgot about me."

"Naw, baby. You gave me a night to remember. Who could forget about that?"

"A night to remember, huh?" I asked.

"Why don't you let me take you out to dinner, and I'll tell you the best damn sex story ever."

I laughed, knowing he was probably talking about our little one night stand. "When?"

"Soon as you're ready."

I smiled. "I'm ready now."

"I'll be there in ten minutes."

I hung up the phone happy as hell. Caddy might not be such a bad guy after all.

****

Caddy picked me up in his very new Cadillac Deville. It was something nice, and I could tell he cherished his ride. That whole evening we spent together was something to remember. He wasn't the jerk I thought he was. He was actually the sweetest man I have ever met. I knew the first date was usually lies, but I liked the game Caddy was kicking to me. He told me a lot about himself, which surprised me because many people don't tell much on first dates. When he took me home, I invited him in and we stayed in my room. We talked more and watched a couple of movies. Of course he was trying to get in my pants, which I expected. I was pretty horny, so I let Caddy have his way with me that night. I was in love all over again.

Me and Caddy had been tight every since that night he took me out to eat. Two and a half weeks had gone by and Caddy was always with me. He made me feel real good. He never left my side and he stayed most nights with me. Last night, we were getting it in and while I was riding the hell out of him, he bust out and told me he loved me. Damn! I guess my plan was going to be easier than I thought.

Caddy was more aggressive than Quentin, and ten times more of a freak. We had sex about four or five times a day. I found out why I was calling his name. I couldn't help but yell. He treated me like we'd known each other forever. Every day he had a surprise for me. I was loving the royal treatment he gave me. It made me wanna marry the man.

It was a Friday evening, around 7:30. I was in the kitchen with Trixsy watching TV. She was baking a birthday cake for her mother because the next day was her birthday and she was throwing her a party at the house. Her mother was like one of us. She was single and acted like she was our age. You couldn't tell her nothing. Her name was Mona, but we called her Monie. Trixsy was making her mom's favorite, red velvet cake. Veronica entered the kitchen, holding her gym bag and car keys. She looked me up and down and frowned.

"I thought you were going to the club with me to watch me dance," she said.

"I'm tired now," I replied, leaning over the counter.

Veronica shook her head. "Caddy wear you out again?"

I laughed a little. "I haven't seen him today."

"Wow. That's a first."

"Did you tell him yet?" Trixsy interrupted.

"Who's him?" We turned to the entrance of the kitchen and Caddy walked in. Perfect timing.

For the past few days he had just been letting himself in as if he lived there. No one minded, but he could just sneak in. I was glad I didn't say anything I wasn't supposed to. Caddy sat on a stool and grabbed an apple out of the fruit basket Trixsy just put out. He sunk his teeth into it and start chomping down.

"You girls talking about me?" he asked with a mouth full of apple.

"No," I quickly answered.

"Then who?" He took another bite. "You got another man?"

I took a deep breath and looked down. I guess I had to tell him. He would think I was seeing someone besides him if I didn't speak up. I looked at Veronica and she got the hint to leave the kitchen. Trixsy stayed while she poured the cake batter into the pan.

I looked at Caddy. "Trixsy didn't cook. Do you wanna go to the dinner?"

"You got something to tell me?" he asked bluntly.

"I'm just hungry," I lied.

"You look like you want to tell me something." He paused and then looked at my body. "Are you pregnant or something?"

Damn, he hit it on the nose. Was he psychic or what? How could he know? I hoped he didn't say it wasn't his.

"Yes," I said in a scared voice.

"Yes?" he repeated. "You're pregnant?"

"Are you mad?"

"Damn, that was quick! I must've got you pregnant on the first night." Caddy set the apple on the table and walked over to me. He grabbed my hand and kissed it. "Baby, I don't know what to say." He looked me in the eye.

"Say you're happy."

"I am....well, maybe." He hesitated. "I..." He was speechless for a long time. His dropped his head and didn't lift it back up.

"Caddy?" I rubbed his knee.

Caddy looked over at Trixsy. "Will you excuse us for a minute?"

Trixsy quickly put the cake in the oven. "Alright, ya'll. I'm leaving."

Trixsy slowly left the kitchen. You could tell she was mad because her ass wanted to be nosy. I didn't mind her staying, but Caddy must've had something important to say, something secretive. In a way, I was frightened. All kinds of thoughts flooded my mind. Was he going to break up with me now? Or even worse, was he going to question my pregnancy?

Soon as Trixsy disappeared from the kitchen, Caddy cleared his throat and then he shook his head from side to side.

"Caddy?" I continued rubbing his knee. "You're mad, huh?"

"Oh, I'm mad." He sighed. "But I'm mad at myself."

"It's my fault, too."

"Naw, baby, not that."

"Not what?"

"I shouldn't of let it get this far." He then smiled at me. "But your fine ass was irresistible." I blushed at that comment. "I don't have any children. I always wanted a baby, but..."

"But what?"

"My wife can't have any kids."

"Your wife!" I yelled. I went hysterical. I jumped up and my chair went backwards. What was I getting myself into? Why did I have to get all the guys that were in relationships? "Why didn't you tell me?" I began to cry. "I actually thought you were the one. You told me you loved me. Why do I have to be the other woman?"

"I do love you!" He grabbed me. "Listen, baby, I don't love her."

"Yeah right. That's what they all say." I moved away from him. "After two weeks, Caddy, you told me you loved me."

"That's no bullshit, I do love you. You're about to have my baby."

I walked away from him, going upstairs. "This can't be!" I yelled.

Caddy chased me upstairs. I pulled away from him when he caught up to me. I instantly thought about Tony and how he did me the same way. I guess Quentin was trying to tell me something.

"I don't love her," he told me. "I haven't slept with her since I met you. I been spending all my time with you, I could care less about her. It's you I want."

"Why didn't you tell me when I called you that day?" I asked, now facing him.

"Truthfully, I just wanted to sleep with you again. I didn't think I'd fall in love with you."

I rolled my eyes. "Caddy, quit using the L word. We only been fucking, and I just happen to get pregnant."

I snatched my arm away from Caddy and I quickly walked to my bedroom. He still followed me, no matter how fast I walked. Once we got inside my room, he closed the door behind him.

"I'll leave Olivia," he said as he walked up onto me.

"So that's her name?"

"Yea. Olivia's my wife."

"I wish you'd told me that night."

"We only been together about three weeks. Aren't you glad I didn't wait a year?"

"You probably would have if I didn't get pregnant."

"So what now?" he asked, totally ignoring my comment.

Caddy stood there with his hands up. He was right though, now what? Caddy couldn't be my baby daddy anymore. He was married. I knew I couldn't turn around and say he wasn't my baby daddy now. What would he think of me? I'd look like a scandalous bitch.

"I can't deal with this right now," I told him. "Me and you should talk later, like after you leave your wife."

"Baby, I promise you, I'm leaving my wife."

"Sorry, Caddy. I can't see you until then."

Caddy looked at me like he was really hurt. He slowly backed away toward the door. He gave me a half smile as he opened the door and walked out. Did

Caddy really love me that much? Naw, he couldn't love me. It had to be the baby that he thought was his. Why did I listen to Jessica? I just ruined this man. Now my stupid ass was in some shit.

I was raging mad at myself. My stomach began to hurt and my eyes teared up, wanting to cry. I walked into the bathroom and sat on the floor next to the garbage can. I wanted to throw up, I felt it coming. I quickly put my head in the trash can since it as closer to me than the toilet. I kept gagging but nothing would come out. When I lifted my head back up my, eyes focused on that pregnancy test I took almost three weeks ago. I cleaned my bathroom regularly, but the trash didn't accumulate much, which made me empty the trash probably just once a month. I grabbed it out of the trash and I stared at it. I don't know why I wanted to stare at it, but I did. Soon as my eyes focused on the test, I swear I wanted to scream, but I didn't. I just slapped my hand on the floor.

"Dammit," I said to myself. "I'm going to kill Veronica."

After all the shit I had been going through, and this stupid test only had one line on it. I tried to stay calm because maybe the second line faded away. It couldn't have faded away that good, the test clearly read one line. There was no sign of a second line at all. I quickly got up and called Veronica on her cell phone. She probably was on her way to the club, but right now, I had to get to the bottom of this.

"Hello?" she answered quickly.

"Veronica," I yelled into the phone. I tried to calm myself before I went off. "Please tell me there were two lines on that pregnancy test I took a couple of weeks ago."

"Why? What's going on?"

"I just looked in the trash in my bathroom and I found the test. There was one line."

"Yeah." She laughed. "Isn't it suppose to have one line?"

I just dropped the phone. Why didn't I look at it after she did? How stupid could Veronica be? I slowly picked up the phone and put it to my ear. All I heard was Veronica's voice at the other end yelling hello. I bit my bottom lip, trying to hold back any tears. I swear I wanted to cry more than ever before.

"Veronica?" I swallowed. "One fuckin' line?"

"A line showed up. That means you're pregnant." She sounded so confident.

"Why did I listen to you?" I sighed. "Well, I was never pregnant. I just told Caddy I was pregnant! Now he says he's going to leave his wife."

"He's married?"

"That was a surprise to me, too. I call myself trying to trick him, and I was never even pregnant."

"I honestly didn't know." I could hear it in Veronica's voice that she felt bad. "Is he there?"

"No, he's gone. Now I have to call him and tell him I'm a liar."

"You know I'm sorry."

"Well," I rolled my eyes, "you didn't know."

"Don't be mad at me."

"I'm not mad at you. I'm mad at myself for fucking men I just met. I need some time to myself right now. I gotta go."

"Okay, I'll see you in the morning."

I hit the end button. I stared at the phone, mean mugging the shit out of it. I sat there thinking about calling Caddy back to the house. What should I tell him? The truth? I mean, what is the truth? I tried to trick him to be my baby's father. That's the truth. Before I could dial his number, I heard Trixsy's voice in my bedroom. I slowly got up and eased into the bedroom. She was standing in the middle of my room, looking at me with her arms folded across her chest.

"Why you break Caddy's heart?" she asked me.

"What he say?"

"He told me he loved you. He downstairs, you know."

"He still here?" I panicked.

"Yeah, now go tell him you're sorry."

"For what," I yelled.

Trixsy walked up to me and pulled me to my bed. She was acting like I was her child and she was scolding me. "Do you see what you got down there?" Trixsy had me by the arm.

I snatched my arm from her and rolled my eyes. "Who? Caddy?"

"Girl, I wish I had a man like Caddy. I mean, I got men that love me and give me things, but Caddy only known you for two weeks and his ass worships the ground you walk on." Then she whispered in my ear. "He's the perfect man to be a father to your baby."

Right when she said that, I broke down into tears. I cried like a baby and Trixsy didn't know why. I fell into her arms, and she held me and stroked my hair. Trixsy didn't say a word to me. She was speechless. All she could do was cradle me. I finally stopped crying and looked at her.

"I'm not pregnant," I told her.

Trixsy looked at me. Her face was so serious. I kept shaking my head no.

"But you took a pregnancy test," she finally said.

"It said you were pregnant."

"Did you see it?"

"No, but Veronica told us."

"I just talked to Veronica." I paused. "She thought one line was pregnant. One line only indicates that it's working."

"Are you sure?"

I shook my head yes. "What am I going to do?"

"I'm so sorry, Azaria. Now I'm mad at Jessica for telling you to be so scandalous."

"Caddy will hate me," I cried.

"No he won't. Just tell him you read the test wrong. I think he'll understand."

I lay back in my bed and cried some more. Trixsy lay next to me talking. Her voice was soothing, but I had no idea what she was saying. My depression took over me and when I got to that point, I was no good. That was probably why I was so sick. It was depression, not pregnancy. I never thought about that until now, because I was getting sick all over again.

I was balled up in a fetus position, crying while Trixsy talked her soothing words. Her voice and my crying eventually put me to sleep.

Chapter Ten

I woke to see Caddy sitting up in my bed. I looked over at the clock and it read 3:45am. I looked back at him, who was watching TV with a Bud Light in his hand.

"Caddy?" I whispered.

He turned around. "Wha's up, baby?"

"What are you doing here?"

"I was waiting for you to wake up."

"Well, it's almost four in the morning."

"I know."

Caddy stood up and walked around the bed. He came over to my side and sat his beer on my nightstand. He then grabbed a small paper bag off the table and sat down on the edge of the bed. He stared at that paper bag for a minute. Something very serious had to be in that bag.

"Trixsy told me," he said, fiddling with the bag.

"She told you what?" I acted like I didn't know what he was talking about.

"You think you're not pregnant."

I was mad at her, it wasn't her place to tell him that. I couldn't believe the way my life was going right now. I wonder what Caddy thought of me. Well, he didn't seem mad about it, maybe that was a good thing. I wondered what he had in that paper bag. I hope he wasn't crazy and wanted to kill me. I probably hurt the poor man feelings and now he wanted to kill me.

"Caddy," I began to explain.

"Baby," he cut me off, " you're just mad and stressed. I know we only been together for two weeks, but I do love you. Don't deny your pregnancy 'cause of me. I'm sorry I didn't tell you about having a wife. I didn't know I would fall in love with you. I promise you, I'm leaving my wife. I'll be by your side from now 'till the very end."

I started to cry. Caddy was the one in denial. He really wanted this baby that I was trying to trick him into fathering and I wasn't pregnant.

"I'm not in denial." I continued to cry. "I took a pregnancy test and it had one line. Negative! I'll take one again and show you. I'm so sorry, Caddy."

Caddy handed me the brown paper bag. "Take it."

I took the bag and opened it. I couldn't believe it, but Caddy really bought a pregnancy test. He really thought I was pregnant. He would've been the perfect father, too.

I got up with the brown paper bag clutched close to me and I walked into the bathroom. Caddy got up behind me and followed. I didn't say anything, even though I would feel uncomfortable peeing while he watched.

Caddy stood in the doorway and watched as sat on the toilet. I pulled the test out the bag and opened the box it was in. I then put the stick of the test under my me and tried to pee. I closed my eyes for a second and when I opened them, Caddy was staring at me, smiling. I shyly smiled back. Finally, I let out a little pee and it went right on the stick. Soon as I was done, I set it on the sink. Caddy went to grab it, but I slapped his hand and he looked at me like I was crazy.

"One line means it's working," I reminded him.

He shook his head in agreement and then grabbed the test. It was too soon for him to look, but I didn't say anything because I knew it was negative.

"Shit," he yelled out.

"I'm sorry, Caddy," I said as I wiped myself and flushed the toilet. "I thought one line meant that I was pregnant."

I washed my hands and then looked at Caddy. He didn't say a word after that outburst. He was leaned against the wall, still looking at the test. He then slid to the floor, still staring at it. I sat against the sink and folded my arms. I felt sad that I led him on. He was very good to me, and I was growing to love him. I hoped he didn't hate me.

Caddy continued staring at that test like it was going to change. After a few more seconds, his facial expression changed. He quickly jumped to his feet and looked at that damn test again, and this time the biggest smile was spread across his face. What was wrong with him?

"Two lines, baby," Caddy yelled out.

"What?" I asked as I walked next to him.

I almost jumped when I saw that there were two lines. I was pregnant! Now what the hell was going on? It had to be some kind of trick. I was dumbfounded, while Caddy picked me up and jumped around with me. He then put me down and continued dancing around to himself. I stayed in that same spot wondering how could it be. Then, I suddenly became worried. *"Who the hell am I pregnant by?"* It had been six weeks since Quentin's death. The first test I took said I wasn't pregnant. Then I slept with Tony three and a half weeks ago. Then it was Caddy the week after. Who was my baby's daddy? I was in even worse shit than I was before. What now?

I walked into the bedroom where Caddy had moved his happy ass to. He settled down when he saw me and lay back on the bed. "C'mere, baby," he whispered in a sexy voice.

I didn't want to. I wanted to cry, but I couldn't let Caddy see that. Not over being pregnant. I just stood there, helpless and confused. Since I wasn't going to Caddy, he stood up and walked to me. He started kissing my neck and worked his magic lips downward. He slipped my pants down and I stepped out of them. Caddy then caressed my thighs while he kissed all over my stomach. Then, his tongue took over, circling and entering my belly button. I grabbed his head and he went down a little further. Next thing you knew, I was grabbing the bed post with one leg over his shoulder and his head between my thighs. Caddy was a man who loved to smell pussy. He would literally be down there forever just savoring the moment. I had to beg him to stop sometimes and tell him to stick that big dick of his in. That was when he had me screaming in ecstasy.

My legs weakened up, and he picked me up and lay me on the bed. I lay there while he took every stitch of my clothes off, then I played with myself while he took off his. When he was done, he lay on a pillow with his dick standing toward the ceiling. I rolled over on top of him and I sat on his manhood. From there, I rode him until I wore him out. Soon as he let a big one go inside of me, I collapsed and fell asleep on his chest.

Chapter Eleven

I went to the doctor three weeks later. I was most definitely pregnant. Good news was, my conception date said the baby couldn't have been Quentin's. Bad news was, I was six weeks pregnant. The baby could be Caddy's or Tony's. My conception date landed sometime between the two of them. My heart said it was Tony's, but my mind says it was Caddy's. Of course, when the baby came into the world it would be obvious who was the father. Tony was a white man with blue eyes and blonde hair, and Caddy wasn't dark-skinned but if the baby was Tony's, he'd definitely know.

The girls knew that the baby could be either man's, and they encouraged me to tell both guys. Caddy would be heart broken, but if I waited till the baby was born, things could get really ugly. I knew I had to do the right thing. Before, I was worried about having a baby's father. Now, I had two different men. They say the Lord works in mysterious ways. I guess this is what I get.

Caddy told his wife, Olivia, everything. Now the bitch was calling me. Her sneaky ass got my number from his cell phone and called asking stupid questions, and then told me they were still sleeping together. I know for sure that was a damn lie because

because Caddy would not leave my side. He had been staying every day and night with me. He did go out once in awhile to handle business, *he says.*

I found out, just like Quentin, Caddy was a drug dealer. He was very well known, too. I found out he owned a 1.5 million dollar home. That's where that bitch Olivia rested her head, but the house was in his name so he could kick her ass out. I thought back to Tony and how I didn't give him a chance. I bet that ex-girlfriend of his was lying. I didn't regret meeting Caddy, but if I gave Tony a second chance, I wouldn't have this problem. So who's my baby daddy?

****

Me and Jessica were in the mall shopping like always. I didn't need a job as long as I had Caddy. He had way more loot than Quentin. I don't think Quentin ever saw the money Caddy had. He never got his hands dirty though. Caddy had an apartment building that he owned and the people that lived there dealt drugs from the place. Caddy sat back and collected.

I had two bags walking through the mall and Jessica had four. She was a real clothes addict. I started getting into all the fancy, designer clothes and with Caddy's money, I never wore an outfit twice. It was crazy, but that's how I became.

We got tired of walking around and sat on a bench. Her ass had to wear some damn four inch stilettos, trying to be cute. I had on some cute, pink and brown Air Max sneakers, so I was straight. While we were sitting there chatting, two good looking guys joined us. One guy was tall and dark-skinned with long dreads that were pulled back into a ponytail and he sat right next to Jessica. I bet her big breast attracted him over. She had on a top that squeezed the hell out of her poor tits. Them thangs just popped right on out.

"I seen you before," he said to Jessica. What a corny ass line, but knowing Jessica she'd fall for it anyway.

"Well, I never seen you," she responded in a flirtatious voice. "I wouldn't forget that face."

He smiled. "You might not remember me, but I remember you."

"From where?"

"You work at the law firm on Peterson Rd."

"So what you doing there?"

"Looking for a lawyer. I talked to Vera."

"She's Mark's secretary. He must've been your lawyer."

"Yea, he was."

"Did you like him?"

"He got me off."

"What?"

"Murder."

"Damn, baby." She gasped. "Serious offense."

"Yea, well, the truth comes out."

"I'm glad Mark got you off. You know, Leon would've been a better attorney. He's the best defense lawyer around."

"Well, that Vera told me different."

"Well of course." Jessica turned her whole body toward him. "She works for Mark."

"And you work for Leon?"

"I do, but I'll be a better defense lawyer. I'm in

school at this moment. I'm almost finished."

"Busy lady, huh?"

"A little. Not too busy." Jessica turned and looked at me. I just nodded my head at her. "Well, we better get going," she said, standing up.

"What's your name?" He stood up with her.

"Jessica. Yours?"

"Antoine."

Jessica extended her hand to Antoine. "It was nice seeing you again, even though I never actually meet you in the office."

"Jessica, if you don't mind, I'd like to take you out sometime."

"Okay." She blushed.

"Maybe tonight, if you're not busy."

Jessica dug around in her Chanel purse and pulled out a business card. "Call me."

"I most definitely will."

"Talk to you then.

Antoine got up along with his quiet friend. They both walked away slowly, glancing back every few minutes. They were talking about us, at least about Jessica.

"Looks like you got a new friend," I told her.

"Girl, he look fuckable. Look at that ass he had. Then, you seen how his jeans looked when he sat down?"

"Damn, girl, you be on it."

"I don't want to get no surprises when he pulls his pants down. I'll embarrass his little dick ass and tell him to go."

"I can't believe you."

"His ass is fine, too, so that's a plus."

"Why don't you settle down? Who knows, this

Antoine guy may be the one."

Jessica looked at me like I was crazy. She rolled her eyes and shook her head. "I can't do that," she said as she looked in her little compact mirror.

"Aren't you tired of fucking different men all the time? Don't you want love?"

"She-it!" She laughed. "I'll be tired fucking the same man. Besides, I don't fall in love."

"You gon' mess around and catch something."

"I use condoms." She looked back at me and licked her lips. "All the damn time."

"What about a family? I know you like kids."

Jessica became serious. "I want a baby more than anything, but I don't think I'm able to have children. I got pregnant once when I thirteen, and twice when I was fourteen. My mama made me get an abortion all three times. After that, I couldn't get pregnant. Then when I was seventeen, I had gonorrhea. I know I can't get pregnant 'cause I had this really nice boyfriend when I was twenty. We tried every day to get pregnant. For a whole year we tried. I don't know if me having all those abortions or diseases did it or what. All I know is I can not have children."

I was speechless after she told me that. This girl had a very promiscuous lifestyle. I bet she didn't know what love felt like. You might as well call her a prostitute, but her hoe ass don't even do it for money.

After that small talk about sex, I tried to change the subject. She just went on some more about having sex. I couldn't believe some of the shit she told me. I kinda figured she was bisexual, but she answered my question when she told me her wild and crazy experiences. Jessica was more than a freak, I didn't know what to call her. I wouldn't judge her though, because she was still a cool person. Maybe she felt I was a good person to talk to or maybe she was just bragging. It was nothing to brag about, 'cause I would just call her ass pure nasty. Her poor pussy got to be all beat up.

Chapter Twelve

We got home a little after five and no one was there. Veronica left us a note saying she was going in early. We already knew Trixsy was out with one of her friends, Stan, who was her her new doctor friend that was married with children. Do you think her scandalous ass cared? No! But I had no room to talk because I was with Caddy and he was married. But then again, Caddy left his wife. In my book he was my man now.

Jessica left me in the living room to go upstairs to get ready for her date. Soon as I sat my butt on the sofa, the door bell rang. I knew it was Caddy because I told him I'd be home around this time. He wanted to cook me dinner and I couldn't wait. I walked to the door and when I opened it, I was more than surprised. I just stood there, looking at his fine ass. I never knew a boy could be so damn good-looking. Tony had it going on. He was looking better than last time, rocking some crisp blue jeans and a Sean John button up.

"Tony?" I looked at him head to toe again.

"Surprise," he said with a half smile.

"What are you doing here?"

"Can I come in?"

I looked around, nervous as hell. I didn't know

what to do. Tony could be my baby's daddy and my other baby daddy was going to be there any minute. I wasn't even ready to tell Tony about my pregnancy yet.

"I guess," I said as I opened the door wider for him to come in.

I watched as he walked in. As he passed me, I inhaled his sexy scent. My panties instantly became wet he smelled so good. Tony waited for me to close the door and when I turned back toward him, he grabbed me and gave me a passionate hug. I enjoyed it, but I had to pull away before I enjoyed it a bit too much.

"I know you received my messages," he said to me.

I looked away. "I did."

"So why haven't you called?"

"I was busy."

"For a month and a half?"

I sighed. "I don't want to get involved with a man who has a girlfriend."

"So you want to believe that bullshit?"

"I don't know. I…"

"Tell me you don't want me," he interrupted. "I know you thought about me."

"Tony," I sighed again, "I'm involved with another guy."

"So you were going to let him be the father of my baby?"

His baby? He shocked me saying that. Damn, how'd he even know I was pregnant? People sure do talk.

"I just found out," I tried to explain.

"Were you going to tell me?"

"Of course."

I quickly turned away from him and walked toward the window. How was I going to tell him the baby I was carrying might not be his? Just thinking about telling him made me cry. How would Tony react to the news? I knew he'd hate me. I wiped my eyes with the tips of my fingers and suddenly felt his touch. He wrapped his arms around me and kissed my neck. I slightly pulled away, so he turned me around. Soon as he looked into my face and saw me crying, he kissed my wet cheeks. Damn, this would be harder than I thought.

"Yo girl Trixsy told my boy, Omar, about you being pregnant," he started to explain. "She don't know that Omar knows me and he had no clue I knew you guys as he was telling me some crazy story about her."

All of a sudden, I began crying even harder. Tony was so sweet, and he just took me into his sexy, warm arms. As much as I loved his touch, I pulled away from him. I was ready to tell him the news.

"I'm not with that lying ass bitch, Tisha," he further explained. "I swear we was over. I don't have any children, and I always wanted some. Baby," he then got on one knee, "I want you to marry me. I know it's soon, but eventually I was going to ask. I want me, you, and the baby to be together as a family."

"Tony, get up," I said, trying to pull him up. "Please don't make this hard for me. I told you I'm seeing someone."

"Fuck him," Tony yelled. "I won't let no other man raise my baby."

I mumbled, "If the baby is yours." If looks could kill, I'd be one dead bitch.

He threw his hands up and walked around the

living room like a mad man. He was on the opposite side of the living room when he punched a hole in the wall. Damn, Veronica was going to kill me. I stayed on the other side, next to the window. I was scared of his ass at this point. Then, he seemed a little calm and looked back over at me.

"You had sex with him before or after me?" he asked.

"One week later."

"One week later? Well, can't the doctor tell you a date or something'?"

"Well, he estimated my conception date in between the time I had sex with you and Caddy."

Tony pounded his balled up fist into his hand. "Why'd you fuck him?"

"You weren't my man!" I snapped. "I could fuck whoever I want."

"So who else could be the father? The mailman, or even some muthafucker standing on the corner? How many other men, Zaria?"

I slapped him across the face. "You don't know what I been through. You was a fuckin' mistake. I was weak and vulnerable at the time. Caddy was a mistake, too. I was drunk."

"So you fell for the guy you got drunk with?"

"It's not even like that."

"So what is it? You wouldn't even give me a chance to explain. But you fall for a man you don't even remember having sex with?"

"You don't know what I remember. It was good, and I was loving every bit of it."

"So you just go out and forget about me?"

"Damn right I did," I lied.

"Yeah whatever. You loved it and you probably

love me."

"Get over yourself. Nobody loves your ass. We just met. It was a one night stand!"

Tony smirked. "You seen my face when you were fucking that Caddy dude?"

I rolled my eyes. "Tony, I don't want us to go no further. All you need to know is this child I'm carrying could be yours."

"Well, I hope not. I hate to have a ho' for a baby mama!"

I couldn't control my actions and I just went at him. I pushed him so hard, he fell back on the sofa. I got on top of him and started slapping, punching, and whatever. I was beating the shit out of him. He finally got a hold of my hands and held them down. I struggled, trying to get out of the bear hold he had me in. Tony was strong and extremely built. He looked like he weighed a good 230.

Tony then reversed our position, and he was standing over me with my arms pinned down over my head. He looked at me for a while with an angry look. I was still struggling, trying to free myself. It was no use, he had me on lock down. I couldn't take it anymore, so I did something I almost regretted, I spit right in his face. Next thing you know, his hands was around my neck, choking the shit out of me. I thought his crazy ass was going to kill me. He must've snapped out of his crazy trance, because he quickly let me go. I grabbed my neck and began coughing.

"Oh, baby, I'm sorry," he apologized. "I didn't mean to do that."

I couldn't get my words out, all I could do was point to the door. He stood there looking pitiful, not taking one step.

"Get...out ...now." I barely got my words out.

"I didn't mean to hurt you. I just..."

"Go now before I call the police."

At that moment, the front door opened. It was Caddy holding two bags of groceries. He saw me on my knees coughing, then he looked up at Tony.

"What the fuck's going on?" he said as he set the bags down. He then looked back over to me. "What happened, baby? You a'ight?"

I quickly stood up and got in front of Tony. I didn't want Caddy whoppin' his ass, even though he deserved it. I watched as Caddy's fists balled up, and I just knew he was ready to blast on Tony.

"Wait, baby." I grabbed Caddy. "I have to explain."

"Did he hurt you?" Caddy asked, not taking his eye off of me.

"He didn't mean to."

I should have lied and said no. Caddy bypassed me and grabbed Tony, but Tony was fast and he slammed into Caddy, knocking him on the coffee table and breaking it. Caddy was lying on the broken table, but kicked Tony, making him to fall back. He then scrambled up and jumped on Tony. He had Tony in a head lock and punching him in the head. Tony came back up and threw Caddy off of him, he was like the Incredible Hulk. Caddy's punches were no joke and every time he punched Tony, it dazed him out. Both of Tony's eyes were swollen.

Jessica entered the living room and saw them going at it. What were we going to do? They were fighting hard and tough. Those two big guys were destroying our entire living room. They broke the big screen TV and entertainment set. The glass curio cabinet shattered. Jessica quickly left and came back with a pitcher of ice cold water. She threw it on them and I quickly grabbed Caddy, as if I was hugging him.

"Please, Caddy!" I cried. "Tony didn't hurt me!"

"He did something to you!" he yelled out of breath.

"No, it's not what it seems."

"She was mines first!" Tony yelled to Caddy. "That's my baby she's carrying."

Caddy pulled away from me and looked me in the face. He was still breathing hard. I could tell he was pissed. "Zaria, please tell me that's not true."

I slowly backed away from Caddy, and there I stood in the middle of them. Tony had a grin and Caddy had a frown. "I was with Tony a week before I was with you." I felt like the biggest whore. Caddy just stood there like he couldn't believe it.

"So you don't know?" Caddy asked.

"No," I answered in shame.

"So why didn't you tell me?"

"I tried. I was waiting for the right time."

"Like now." He then looked over at Tony. "Did you know about me?"

"Naw," he answered. "She just told me."

Caddy wiped the blood from off his lips. He looked so sad. What the hell did I do?

"Caddy," I started, "we were drunk that night and didn't use no condom. I mean, I didn't mean to sleep with you. It just happened. Yes, the baby could be yours." I then looked at Tony, "Or yours. I'm sorry to both of you. I'll get an abortion if..."

"No!" Caddy interrupted. "If it's mine, I want the baby."

"So do I," Tony agreed.

"I swear you two are the only possibilities."

From the corner of my eye, I could see Jessica slowly exit the room. I guess she knew it was her time to go. Tony walked over to the sofa and sat down. Caddy walked in circles.

"I apologize for earlier, Zaria," Tony said sincerely. "I was just pissed off."

"What happened earlier?" Caddy wanted to know.

"I slapped him a couple of times, then spit in his face. That's when he choked me."

Caddy grinned a little. "Well damn. Sorry, baby, but I probably would've choked you, too."

I ignored his little comment. "Look, I didn't do this alone, nor did I do this on purpose. I mean, you guys wasn't thinking about condoms neither."

"Honestly," Tony began, "I know that's my baby. I never pulled out till I completely unloaded my stuff."

"I came inside you, too," Caddy bragged.

"You was drunk," Tony snapped on him. "You probably wore a condom."

"I wasn't that damn drunk!"

"Please, you guys." Now they were both acting childish, and it was getting to me. "This is harder for me than it is for you. I'm carrying the baby, and this situation stresses me out."

"Well take care of my baby, Zaria." Caddy limped to the door. "Call me when you go in labor."

"Caddy, wait," I cried out. "You can't leave me. This is not all on me."

"I can't deal with another man in this relationship."

"I'm not with Tony. I'm with you. Please don't do this to me."

"What am I suppose to do?"

"Be there for me," I begged.

"You got homeboy. I'm out."

I looked over at Tony, and he had this 'I won' grin on his face. I wasn't going to beg for Caddy, but I didn't want him to leave me. Oh, what the hell, fuck him! I liked Caddy a lot. The past few weeks we spent together meant a lot to me. It almost felt as if I loved him. I even wanted Caddy to be the father, not Tony. He was dangerous, not baby daddy material. After tonight, I was afraid of his crazy ass and I'd remind myself to never get on his bad side. I stood there watching Caddy walk out my door and the look on my face told it all, I was back to depression again. I looked over at Tony, then I did what I always did, run! I ran upstairs to my bedroom, locked my door behind myself, and plopped on the bed. I could hear Tony pounding on my door but I was not letting him in. I was mad at myself, not him, but I refused to give in. I was going to hide from the world till I went in labor.

Chapter Thirteen

I couldn't stay in my room that long. Veronica talked me out the next morning, but it didn't last long when Tony came back. I didn't let him say one word before I went back to hide out in my room. That was two hours ago, and I wasn't going back out there. I had just finished watching a good ass movie on Lifetime when I heard Veronica yell my name through the door.

"What?" I was annoyed.

"Get the phone," she told me. "It's some guy."

I rolled my eyes, knowing it was one person. "Where's Tony?"

"He's downstairs waiting on you to come out."

Damn, I guess it was Caddy calling me, but I didn't want to talk to him either. I didn't like how he left me. I would not forgive him.

"Tell Caddy I don't want to talk to him," I whined, sounding like a baby.

"It's not Caddy. Will you pick up your phone?"

Who else could it be? Now I was curious. None of my family knew where I was except my mom and she wouldn't tell anyone. I was still hiding out from them crazy ass killers.

"Ask him who it is," I said as I listened patiently

through the door. I heard Veronica ask the caller for his name. It sounded as if he was giving her a hard time. Something wasn't right and I was scared. I got off my bed and walked to the door. I pulled the door open and saw Tony leaning up against the wall. Veronica had a puzzled look on her face.

"He says he's friends with Quentin." She handed me the phone.

"What?" After taking the phone, I slowly put it to my ear and listened for a second. "Hello?" I whispered.

"Did you miss me?" the deep voice on the other end asked.

I swear my heart dropped to the pit of my stomach. He was the last person I thought would find me.

"Umm, wrong number," I said, and was about to hang up.

"Wait, Azaria! Let me talk to you first." He paused. "You listening?"

"What?"

"I'm not the one you should be running from. I mean, you are running from me, right?"

"Why are you following me?"

"You have bigger problems than me following you. Your biggest problem is right under your nose, and you have no fuckin' idea. This wasn't planned, but I'm loving it. Oh yeah, I almost forgot, congratulations on your pregnancy."

"Oh, you son of a bitch!"

"I'll stay in touch." He laughed an evil laugh and then hung up.

I dropped the phone and looked at Veronica. I was speechless and scared. Tony picked up the phone and walked me over to my bed.

"Who was that?" Tony asked.

"I don't know." I stared off in space. "I mean, I do, but I don't know....." I began crying.

"What's wrong, Zaria?" Veronica asked. "Do you know that guy?"

"What did the caller ID say?"

"Private."

Just then the phone rang again and Tony answered it before I could say no. "Who is this?" He paused. "What the fuck you want with her?" He paused again. "If I find out who you are, I'll kill your ass!"

Tony hit the end button and looked over at me. He sat the phone down and shook his head.

"Whoever the fuck that was, he's following you. He said my name. I think you need to call the police. I don't know what's going on, but I don't like this shit one bit."

"Fine, call the police," I yelled out. "I think I know who that was."

"Who!"

"One of the guys that killed Quentin."

"Oh shit." Veronica gasped. "How'd he find you?"

"Who's Quentin?" Tony questioned.

I looked over at Tony. "He was my boyfriend who was murdered."

"Whoa." Tony eased down onto my bed. "That's scary."

"Will you call the police, now?"

Tony picked up the phone and called the police. Within ten minutes they arrived at the house. We took them into the dining room and began the questioning began. I was having second thoughts about talking to the police because I knew that guy was watching me from somewhere, but it was too late. I told the police everything that happened in New York, from Quentin being murdered to them trying to kill me. I left out a big part that no one else knew about except me and those faceless guys. I guess it all worked out for me because they were going to provide me round the clock protection for awhile, courtesy of Tony since his uncle was a sergeant at the station.

****

I did the one thing I didn't want to do since I was supposed to be mad at him, I let Tony back into my life. I needed a man right now, and Tony was there. He was always at my house, day and night. It was cool, but I dearly missed Caddy. One night when Tony left my house, I did it. I called Caddy. I was lying across my bed when I dialed his cell number.

"Yeah, what's up?" he said into the phone.

I hesitated. "Hey."

"Who's this?"

I sighed. "Me, Zaria."

"Oh, what's up?"

"I was just thinking about you."

"And not yo' white boy?" He was harsh.

"I'm always thinking about you."

"Before or after you have sex with him." I could hear the coldness in is voice.

"I'm not having sex with Tony."

"So who you having sex with? I ain't been hittin' it."

I sighed. "I can go without, but I bet you been busy."

I could hear him laugh a little. "Actually, I have been busy. No wife, no wifey, no worries. I'm a single man now."

I didn't respond to Caddy. I was so damn mad at my sensitive ass. Why did I call this fool? Maybe because I wanted him in the bed with me, I missed him so much. Why did he have to act so stupid about the situation? Didn't he know I loved him?

"You still there?" He interrupted my thoughts.

"I'm sorry to bother you, I just wanted to say hi."

"Well," he began, "what's been going on?"

I hesitated. "Things haven't been too good."

"What's wrong?" I heard worry in his voice. "The baby alright?"

"The baby is fine. A couple of weeks ago I received a phone call from the man that murdered my ex. I think he wants to kill me."

"Someone's after you?"

"I think so. Police has been outside the house and monitoring our house phone. I been okay since."

"Why didn't you call me?"

"I didn't think you cared."

"Baby, I care." He sounded sincere. "I just needed some time. I told you I loved you, and I meant it. Honestly, I been waiting for this phone call. I was too stubborn to call you. I'm so sorry, baby."

"I was so afraid you'd hang up on me."

"Never. You probably been under a lot of stress. Do you want to come over here?"

"Your house? But what about Olivia?"

"I told you I don't have a wife no more. She left after I told her about you. She moved to Washington with her folks. I was trying to tell you about me and Olivia until I met Tony that night."

"Sorry 'bout that."

"So, do you think you can get away from the police?"

"I'll try to sneak out the back door. Meet me in the alley in thirty minutes."

"I'll be there."

After I hung up my cell phone, I lay back on my bed and smiled like I never smiled before. I was so happy I got my man back. Caddy really loved me. After all this time, I just thought he forgot about me.

I told the girls about my scheme to be with Caddy for the night and they were going to make sure to cover for me. Jessica was going to distract the two officers that covered the shift. The boys were sitting out in their car doing Lord knows what and she eased out there in a sexy ass chemise that was practically see through. She was going inviting them in for dinner. They were all smiles as we watched through an upstairs window at how they followed Jessica. Once they were all in the kitchen, I snuck out the front door and ran toward the alley which was across our backyard. Caddy's black Cadillac was sitting there, shining on it's 22 inch rims. Soon as I got in, he licked his big, juicy, wet lips and looked me up and down.

"Damn, you are the most beautiful woman I ever laid eyes on. I can't believe I went this long without seeing your sexy ass. You are looking good."

"Thank you, baby, you look good, too."

He leaned over to me and sucked in my lips, kissing me wildly. Caddy's lips tasted good, too. I couldn't wait to taste his dick. Damn, I was horny.

It would be my second time at Caddy's house and

it was still beautiful. He lived like a celebrity. I knew he was a hustler, but I never got into asking him about it. I was used to drug dealers. Didn't want me one, but that bad boy image turned me on. Maybe that's what made Tony so sexy. Although he was a stripper, he had that thug mentality.

Soon as we entered his house he excused himself. I helped my self to the living room area, and a couple of minutes later, Caddy came back with two glasses filled with wine.

"Don't worry, baby," he said as he handed me mine. "Yours is sparkling' wine."

After I watched Caddy down his, I brought my glass to my lips taking a small sip. He wasted no time taking me by the hand, and pulling me up off the sofa.

"I missed you, baby," he said as he led me into his bedroom. I knew he missed this pussy. It was good before I got pregnant, so I knew it was the shit now.

When we got into his bedroom, he took the glass out my hand and set it on a near by dresser. Then, he stood in front of me, feeling on my body.

"You tired?" he asked me.

"No."

"You want to take a shower with me?"

I smiled. "Yes."

"I don't think you've seen my shower. It's huge."

"The more room, the better."

Caddy grabbed my hand, and led me into his master bathroom. He had a huge Jacuzzi, and opposite of that was the huge shower. It looked as if it could fit about five people. He started the shower and I stripped down. I got in before him and stood under the umbrella sized nozzle. I looked through the crystal clear glass door and watched Caddy strip down. He walked away for a minute and brought back two small wash cloths and some body wash. Soon as he got in he began to wash my body and I closed my eyes, loving the feeling. Then, I did him the same way. It was hard washing his dick without wrapping my lips around it, it looked so damn good. I loved how the soap glistened all over it. Before I could even try to get freaky with him, he grabbed the wash cloth out my hand and threw it on the floor. He placed both my hands against the wall, with my backside towards him. I could feel his hands exploring every inch of my body. I arched my back and stuck my perfectly round ass out until it touched his manhood. He grabbed my hips and slowly eased it in. I immediately grabbed a hold of the railing in the shower and moans escaped my lips. Caddy rocked my hips back and forth in a slow rhythm, and it felt so damn good. The water dropping on our bare bodies made our sex more exciting. Caddy liked to talk a lot of shit while he was getting his dick wet. I liked it, too. I never actually did it until I met Caddy, he had me answering him. He kept yelling, "Whose pussy is this?" Of course I yell back, "Yours daddy." I meant it, too.

Caddy pulled out and turned me around. He picked me up and started fucking me up against the tiled wall. He turned into an animal, and was ramming his dick in. Did he forget I was pregnant? I screamed out in pleasure, 'cause I liked it hard and rough myself. Caddy let out a loud groan and we were both ready to cum. He pulled out, and shot it all over my stomach and thighs. Why would he want to pull out now? The damage was done, I was already pregnant.

Caddy gently let me down and he sat down in the shower. He was breathing hard and had the biggest smile on his face. I quickly grabbed the wash cloth and body soap, and washed my body off. I sat down in the shower next to him and he grabbed my hand and looked over at me. The water was dripping down his face and he was still sexy.

"Damn, baby." He continued to smile "That was good."

"You act like you ain't had none in awhile."

"I haven't. I lied to you on the phone. I was just trying to get you jealous."

"Well it worked."

"Every time my phone rang I was hoping it was you."

"Really?" I leaned over and kissed him.

"I missed yo' fine ass."

Caddy stood up and washed himself real quick and then he turned the shower off. We got out and he gave me a big dry towel. Caddy pulled me up close to him and held me in his arms.

"I'm afraid, Zaria," he confessed.

"Afraid of what?"

"I want this baby so bad."

I looked away from Caddy and suddenly felt embarrassed. Besides that, I felt so bad. Two men wanted to be my baby's father, when in the end, one will get hurt. He turned my face back toward him.

"I was mad that day. You were right, it's not just you, baby. I'm gonna be by your side no matter what." Caddy then shook his head. "And maybe that punk ass white boy, what made you want to be with him? Were you always attracted to white guys?"

"Tony was my first white guy. When I met him it wasn't the color of his skin, he's very popular, and," I paused, "he's sexy. He's a stripper."

Caddy laughed. "A stripper?!"

"I was curious."

"Can he work it?"

"Caddy!" I couldn't believe he asked me that. "Why would you ask me that?"

"Well, now I'm curious."

"Do you really want to know?"

"I won't get mad. I know he ain't got shit on me."

"You're sounding like you're in high school."

"Well, let's pretend that I am. Is he any good?"

"He's good, but not better than you."

"You don't plan on being with him again, do you?"

I knew that question was a trick. I took a deep breath and walked away from Caddy. I walked around his large bathroom as he looked at me, waiting for an answer.

"Tony's been by my side since you left me. Not once has he tried to have sex with me, and it was never on my mind. We developed a real good friendship. I don't want to loose that."

"Do he love you?"

"He never said he did."

"Was he staying the night?"

"No, we just hung out. We did what friends do. Caddy, you are the only man I want to be with. I don't want to loose you because I'm friends with Tony."

Caddy sighed. "A'ight, baby, that's cool, but what if the baby is his?"

"Will you still stay with me?"

"Will you leave me for him?"

"Never." I walked back over to Caddy, holding my arms out. "Come here."

Caddy walked up to me and picked me up. My towel fell while he carried me into his bedroom. He lay me on his bed and we started again with our lovemaking. Caddy blew my mind. I was so glad we were back together. I just hoped Tony being around wouldn't interfere.

Chapter Fourteen

I was now five months pregnant and had a little belly. Not much, I could pass for having a beer gut. My ass was looking more like Deelishis from *'Flavor Of Love'* and my tits seemed to look bigger as well. Jessica would make comments about my pregnant body, but that bitch was just jealous and I let her smart ass comments go in one ear and out the other. I was loving the pounds the baby gave me. As long as my ass didn't start looking wide, I was fine.

Caddy was pressuring me to move in with him. As much as I wanted to, I couldn't do it, at least not yet. I wanted to have my baby first. If the baby was Tony's I would want him to come around and visit but I couldn't do that living under Caddy's roof. Dealing with Caddy and Tony right now was crazy anyway. Caddy usually stayed the night with me and Tony would pop up with all kinds of gifts for the baby. Him and Caddy were getting into many confrontations. The last one was about naming the baby. Tony had a few names picked out and Caddy was angry at him for even thinking about choosing a name for HIS baby. I had to sit them two of them down and talk it out, especially with Tony. He was getting ahead of himself picking out names and buying gifts. I didn't want either of them planning anything until the baby was born.

I had to put Tony in his place. He was thinking if the baby was his, so was I. I told him I was staying with Caddy no matter what. I understood Tony was there when Caddy left me and he stayed by my side when I was getting those strange phone calls, which I haven't had since. The police stopped monitoring our phones and staying in front of our house. I appreciated everything Tony had done for me, but all I was to him was his friend.

I was always embarrassed when it came to going to the doctor's office because they both wanted to go. I preferred to go went alone or with one of the girls, but the guys wouldn't take no for an answer. I had to suffer the embarrassment of having two men with me.

We were going to find out the sex of the baby. Tony would always meet me and Caddy at the doctor's office, but this time Tony rode with us in my truck. Apparently, his truck was getting work done. I didn't mind, but Caddy was pissed the entire time. I pulled up in front of the office and we all got out. Tony was quick to open the office door for me, but closed it in Caddy's face.

"You mutherfucker," I heard Caddy mumble under his breath.

I didn't expect what happened next when Caddy shoved Tony against the wall. Thank God no one really noticed because Tony caught his balance and played it off, but the look on his face said he wanted to fuck Caddy up. Tony had a really bad temper, and I watched him as he took a deep breath and calmed down. He knew better than to start a fight in the doctor's office. Besides, it was his fault. He shouldn't have closed the door in Caddy's face.

I checked in as Caddy and Tony both sat down, leaving an empty seat in between them for me. When I finished, I sat down and observed the other patients. There were two other couples in the waiting room, and next to Caddy sat a young girl who looked to be about due. She was a pretty girl, maybe around fifteen or sixteen. She was all alone. I bet her baby daddy claimed it wasn't his. Poor little girl.

Caddy sat there flipping through a parenting magazine while Tony stared at the aquarium in the wall. I usually felt really uncomfortable having two men waiting with me, but for some reason, I didn't feel that way today. Maybe because I realized I had two supportive guys wanting to be my baby's father when that poor little girl had no one.

Tony looked over at one of the couples and smiled. When the guy looked up at him, I just knew friendly ass Tony was going to talk. He always made conversation first.

"You having a boy or girl?" he asked the guy.

"We want to be surprised," the man responded.

"I guess that's good." Tony then looked over at me and gave me a look. I knew he wanted to be surprised, too.

"How 'bout yourself?"

"Oh, we find out today."

The guy's woman then looked over at me. "How far along are you?

"Twenty weeks."

She smiled. "I'm seven months and look ten. You hardly look pregnant, lucky you."

I just smiled. After that we were all quiet, until the other woman whose just been watching us spoke up.

"We're having a boy," she said with excitement.

"Congratulations," I said.

"I want a boy," Tony said.

"I want a girl," Caddy said as he looked at Tony.

"Naw, a boy would be better. You got to be overprotective of a girl. I don't wanna kill no little boys for hurting my daughter's feelings." Tony laughed a little.

Everyone looked at him and didn't say a word. They probably thought he was crazy. Then again, they probably was wondering which one was with me.

"Well, I'm having a girl," the young girl finally said. "I'm like two days overdue. Hopefully, the doctor tells me I can have this baby now."

"Wow." I was amazed at how big she was. "I hope I don't go over."

"You look like Jerry's brother," the girl said to Caddy. "Jerry's my baby's daddy."

"I don't know no Jerry. Where he at?"

I nudged Caddy on his side and he apologized. That was none of his business. She probably didn't want to talk about it.

"It's okay. He don't think the baby is his so he don't come around. He even got some other girl pregnant and left her, too."

"Damn," Caddy whispered.

"Yeah, he's an asshole," the girl said.

The first woman I spoke to earlier spoke up to the girl. "You just stay strong. I was a single mom at fourteen. I'm thirty now, pregnant with my fifth child, and married to a successful real estate agent. I'm a pharmacist. Don't you give up."

"Thank you." The girl smiled.

Five children? Whoa. They sound like they doing

it though. Real estate agent. Pharmacist. I didn't even have a damn job. Both possibilities weren't good role models for my child. Why wasn't I attracted to a lawyer or doctor? I got one that takes his clothes off for a living and another that's a drug dealer.

The nurse came out and called Lolita, which was the young girl. We all wished her luck as she waddled to the back to see the doctor.

Soon as the door closed one of the guys started talking to Tony.

"Is this your first child?" he asked.

"Yeah."

"Being a dad is really exciting. The father of that little girl don't know what he's missing."

"That's true," Tony replied. "I'm looking forward to being a father."

I started to become nervous. Tony might say shit that could piss Caddy off. I didn't want that to happen but I knew him just talking about being a father would piss Caddy off. Thank God Caddy kept quiet the entire time.

When we finally went to the back, I made both Caddy and Tony stand outside the door until I put that stupid gown on. I wouldn't mind Caddy, but Tony's dick would've got hard watching me. I definitely did not want that to happen. You never know when it comes to his freaky ass.

The ultrasound was so fun to look at, and believe it or not, I could see the baby real good. Usually people were asking where was the head, the feet, or the hands, but since I was looking at a 3-D ultra sound, I swear you I could just about see the baby's features.

"Your baby is tall," Dr. Morrison told me.

"Like me," Tony boosted.

"I'm tall, too." Caddy pointed to the ultra sound. "That's my nose."

"That's my head," Tony added.

"You guys, please!" I was getting stressed. "You can't tell yet. The baby is still growing. Just listen to the doctor and be quiet."

They both sat back in their chairs and I sighed.

"So," Dr. Morrison started. "Do you want to know the sex?"

"Yeah," Both men said.

The doctor laughed a little. He thought Caddy and Tony were so funny. I told him my situation at my first appointment. He loved the fact that both guys knew and wanted to be apart of my baby's life. Every visit Caddy and Tony argued and Dr. Morison just laughed. He knew Tony wanted a boy and Caddy a girl. I just want a healthy baby.

"Well," Dr. Morrison looked at us all, "I'm pretty sure she's a girl."

"A girl," Caddy shouted. "Yes!"

"What?" Tony pointed to the screen. "Isn't that the little thang?"

"Sorry, Tony. That's the umbilical cord."

"Can't be."

"It is what it is, playa." Caddy stood up, and did a little dance. "Face it, homie, I make beautiful little girls, yo' ass shoot blanks."

Caddy started laughing hard and Tony was turning red. He was about to blow. The more Caddy laughed, the more pissed Tony got.

"You wanna be a fuckin' smart ass?" Tony was angry.

Caddy smiled. "I eat bitches like you for dinner.

Try me, playa."

Tony pounded his fist into the wall, putting a big ass hole the size of a head into it. Then he walked out, slamming the door.

"Ohmigod, Dr. Morrison." I sat up looking at that hole. "I'm so sorry. I'll pay for that."

Caddy dug into his pocket and I watched as he pulled out a wad of cash. He peeled off five hundred dollar bills.

"If that don't do it, call me. That's all I brought today besides the bill for this visit."

Dr. Morrison smiled like always. "I think this will be good."

He took off his gloves, took the money, and put it in his pocket quickly. He washed his hands and returned to us.

"Well, congratulations, you're having a girl. If you ask me, I think she looks like you, Calvin."

Caddy shook his hand. "Thanks, doc."

Soon as Dr. Morrison left, I had it out with Caddy.

"You two are so childish. Ya'll teasing each other like some damn third graders. I am so tired of both of you. I'm going to have to start coming to the doctor alone."

"I'm sorry, but you know he always starting shit with me."

"I think you should tell Tony sorry. You threatened him when you said you'll eat him for dinner. That's like killing someone, Caddy."

"I'm not telling his punk ass sorry, and he best believe he's messing with the wrong nigga. He don't know me!"

"Caddy, if this baby is his, you have to deal with him."

"Never, if it's his, I'm out!"

"What?" I yelled out. "But you said...."

"Fuck what I said! Now I'm saying I'm out if the baby's white."

Caddy left the room, leaving me to look like an idiot and cry. I cried while I got dressed. Soon as I was done, I went to the receptionist and found out my bill was paid. I thought it was Caddy that did it until she said Tony took care of it. As angry as he was, I was shocked that he stopped at the desk to pay the bill. I looked around for both of them and couldn't find either. They must've walked home. I sat in my car for probably a good thirty minutes crying and thinking. If Caddy wanted to act like that, then fuck him. I would do this alone, I didn't need neither of them. I wasn't going back with Caddy, even if he did apologize. Both him and Tony was starting to hate men, at least baby daddies.

Chapter Fifteen

It was 9:30pm, and I was so depressed. I had to get over being over depressed all the time. Caddy never called, and I sure wasn't calling him. Tony left leave a message on my phone apologizing to me. He was a sweet guy with a bad temper. I was going to call him back, but he had already left for work.

Veronica had the night off so her and Jessica were going out. Trixsy was in Puerto Rico with one of her men. I think it was the cop, Roger, that she met while he was watching our house. The bad part was, Roger was married. What a dog. Trixsy didn't care, she had Roger eating out the palm of her hand. He'd do any and everything for her, including drinking her dirty ass bath water. Just last week she showed us the princess cut, diamond ring he bought her. She claimed he proposed, I guess his stupid ass forgot he was married.

I was in the walk-in closet helping Jessica and Veronica find something to wear. I was good at matching clothes up, the fashion expert. I should've been a designer, but I was after men and their pockets instead of college.

I swear they are naked every time they go out. Especially hot ass Jessica. Miss thang always had to rub ice on her nipples before going out because she always wanted them to be rock hard. I felt like joining them. I don't know where they were going, but I was going to.

I was looking for something to wear. "I helped ya'll find something, now help me."

"You're going with us?" Veronica asked with excitement in her voice.

"I might."

"What's got into you?" Jessica spoke up. "We go out every weekend, and you never go with us."

I sighed. "Well, I broke up with Caddy today."

"Are you serious?" Veronica walked up to me and gave me a hug.

"I don't care," I lied. "He's an asshole. Him and Tony are forever arguing. You know, Caddy said if the baby was white, it's over."

"Do you blame him?" Jessica pranced over to the shoes wearing nothing but a thong. "You and Caddy are together, and Tony's always around being a third leg. Caddy's jealous and I don't blame him. I'd leave your ass, too."

I rolled my eyes. "Everyone knows Tony and I are just friends."

"You may think so, but Tony want your ass bad."

"Well, Caddy's the asshole if you ask me," Veronica said, rubbing my back. "He promised you he'd be there no matter what, now he wants to back away. What if the baby is his? He's going to try to run right back into your life."

"I want to forget both of them," I said. "I'm going to have fun tonight."

"What's fun to you?" Veronica looked at me with a strange look on her face.

"Don't worry, girl, I won't drink or have sex with any strangers."

"I just want to know what a pregnant woman gonna do at the club."

"Dance!"

****

We were all dressed and ready to go at 11:30. Jessica drove us around to a couple of clubs. She seemed to be looking in the parking lots and if she didn't see any Benzs or Bentleys, then she wasn't stopping. So we kept riding around to the next club and listening to music.

"Zaria, honey, don't be mad," Jessica announced.

"Why would I be mad?"

"'Cause I want to see some big dicks swinging in my face."

I laughed at my nasty friend. "And why would I be mad about that?"

Her and Veronica both looked at me. Veronica shrugged her shoulders and Jessica had a smirk on her face.

"We're going to Palamont."

Oh, now I get it. She thought I didn't want to see Tony. I didn't care. He was cool with me, just not Caddy.

"I'm not mad." I smiled at the thought. "I haven't seen his dick in so long. But I will not fuck him."

Jessica was quick to make a U-turn. The club was only two blocks away, and we were there in no time.

I walked into the club behind Jessica and Veronica. It was a special night and all we had to pay was ten dollars a piece. The club was so packed we couldn't find a seat, so we just stood along the wall watching the scenery. Soon as I saw who was on stage,

I damn near froze. It was Tony and another woman freakin' it. She was fully dressed in a skimpy black dress, backing her ass up on his big dick. He barely had that covered with a shiny silver thong. The club wasn't that strict. I never heard of any sex going on, but there was a lot of touching and licking . Tony done told me some stories. I could never do what these women did, get up on stage and touch all over them, let the guys touch all over them. They were plain nasty. I was a freak behind doors.

I grabbed the girls and walked toward the stage. We stood to the side, watching Tony work the shit of that girl. Tony soon noticed us and he smiled. I gave him a little smile back.

It was a couple of minutes later and his time was done. Soon as he exited the stage, another stripper, Lundon, got up there with his crazy self. Lundon was just like Jessica, they both were the biggest whores. And yes, Lundon slept with Jessica. She was probably planning on sleeping with him tonight, because her happy ass ran straight up to the stage shaking some dollars. They would never work in a relationship, they were too much alike. She claimed she'd drop every other man for him because she couldn't resist his mocha brown skin and green eyes. He was so exotic looking. Lundon was just as fine and sexy as Tony and they were extremely popular amongst the ladies. One problem with Lundon though, his crazy ass couldn't dance. You'd swear Lundon was white and Tony was the soul brotha.

Veronica disappeared into the private rooms to snatch her up a dancer. I stood there watching Jessica put them dollars in his g-string. I was startled when I heard a voice.

"Did you like what you see?" he said.

I turned around and it was Tony. He had no shirt on, showing his big, oily chest and that six pack. He had it goin' on. He had on blue jeans on with no belt and his pants sagged a little, and you could tell he had nothing on underneath them jeans. I stared at his trimmed up blond trail leading to the magic kingdom.

"Hey, sweetheart, my face is up here." He caught me drooling over him and. He laughed and I blushed.

"Sorry," I said. "You were good up there."

He grabbed my hand. "Let me show you more."

"Excuse me?"

"Private dance. I wanna show you what I really can do. Besides, I'm trying to avoid Shaqueitta over there."

I looked behind Tony at the bar, and saw a tall, black woman with a blond wig at the bar. She had way too much make-up on, looking like a drag queen. She was so ugly, I'd probably run, too.

"Go head and let Shaqueitta have you. I don't have any money to be paying for a dance."

"You know I'd do anything for you. It's on me. Besides, Shaqueitta's a man."

"Ooohhh!" No wonder he was running away. Tony led me to the back of the club where there were a couple of doors. He opened one, and it looked like a small VIP room. It was so beautiful, and elegant looking, too elegant to be in a strip club.

"These rooms are for the high paying customers," Tony said as he closed the door behind us.

I sat down in the red velvet sofa and Tony sat close. He took it upon himself to lift my shirt, exposing my protruding belly. I wasn't uncomfortable so I let him do it. He rubbed it and even kissed it.

"Did you get my message?" he asked me.

"I did."

"I'll always be there for you whether the baby's mine or not. I'm just going to...." He paused. "I wont come around you often. I need to respect you and Caddy's relationship. I been causing too many problems."

"You don't have to worry about him. We sort of broke up."

"Really?" He sounded happy. "Sorry. Was it because of me?"

"No. He's just acting stupid."

"You don't need him anyway. You got me."

"Tony I..."

"For real, baby," He was serious. "I'm here. Always. You wouldn't have to deal with Caddy if you never left me. You should've trusted me."

"I was afraid of getting hurt again. I've been hurt a lot in the past."

Tony grabbed my hand. "The past. Speaking of the past, you never told me much about Quentin and his murder."

"What's there to talk about? Quentin was my ex boyfriend, and he's now dead."

"Were you with him before he died?"

"Yes. We were living together."

"I bet that was hard."

"We just got back together the day he was killed. He was lying and cheating on me. I finally forgave him."

"If you don't mind me asking, what happened?"

"Some guys robbed him a couple months before he was killed. Well, he found out who robbed him and him and his cousin killed him." I took a deep breath.

"So, the other guys came back for Quentin. Not only to kill him, but to rob him again. They practically cleaned him out the first time so I don't know where they think he had more money. They came into our house one morning and tortured him dead. I was in the bathroom when I heard the whole thing."

"Did you see their face?"

"Not really. That's why I left and moved here. No one knows where I moved to, except my mother. She don't know where Veronica lives, she just knows I'm with her." I paused. "I'll call her from my cell phone once in awhile to let her know I'm okay. One day we'll reunite. She understands I need to protect myself. Soon as all this clears, maybe I'll go back to see my family."

"So what if this never clears? I mean, someone did track you down."

"I know." I sighed.

"They shouldn't be worried about you. You never seen their faces, right?"

I turned my head away so Tony wouldn't see my cry. I did have a little secret, a secret that forced me to go into hiding. I never knew they'd be after me. I just thought they killed Quentin, maybe found more cash and they were done. They knew I never saw their face, so why worry.

"You alright, Zaria?" he asked.

"No." I cried my heart out. "They won't stop until they find me. Something else happened."

"What?"

I turned my body toward Tony and prepared myself to tell him my story.

Chapter Sixteen

The next week after Quentin's murder and all the questioning, I went to my mother's house and stayed with her. I went into the guest bedroom and tried to get some rest. I was planning on staying there until I died, I thought loosing Quentin was the end of me. My phone kept ringing off the hook, but I wouldn't dare to answer it. I figured it was family and friends checking up on me. My mom peeped her head inside the room to let me know she was running to the store. I didn't respond to her, so she just closed the door and left.

After about twenty minutes, my door opened. I never heard my mother's voice, but I could feel the presence of someone. I pulled the blanket from over my head and saw my worse nightmare. Before I could scream, two masked guys grabbed me. One of them duck tapped me up and the other held me down. They threw the blanket over me, covering my entire body. I could feel one carrying me and he moved fast. Thirty minutes has passed and I knew they had taken me to another location. I heard car doors slamming, someone breaking glass, and deep male voices. Soon as they removed the blanket, I saw that I was back at my house. The guy with the black ski mask and the red baseball cap gently removed the duck tap from my lips. The other guy had on a ski mask, too, with a black cap. He was the more violent one, and talked the most. He got in my face, grabbing me by the neck.

"Show us where he stashed the money and we won't hurt you," black cap spoke. "That's not his money, it was mine. I want it back."

"I....I..." I was so frightened, and did not want to give them all Quentin left me. "I have about fifteen thousand, but it's not here."

"Fuck the fifteen thousand. That's your shit! That nigga stole my money, and I want it back. Millions!"

I knew nothing about Quentin having millions of dollars. He wasn't ballin' like that. I been with Quentin for ten years, and although he had money, it was never a million dollars. He would've told me. I would've known.

"Fuck it!" black cap yelled out. He looked toward his partner. "You still want to fuck her ass. Maybe then she'll tell me where he put that money."

"No!" I yelled out. "Please don't. I'm telling you the truth when I say I don't know. I never knew he had that kind of money."

"Maybe he told the other bitch," red cap said under a muffled voice. "She the innocent one."

"How's he gonna hide ten million dollars in front of her? She gotta know," black cap argued.

"Just tear this house up," red cap demanded. "I need some bonding time."

Black cap laughed, and I knew exactly what he meant. He was really gonna try to fuck me. Soon as black cap left the room, red cap suddenly turned evil. He pulled out a gun and slowly circled it around my face, and eased it down towards my breast. He ripped my tank top off and my tears just fell.

"You're so beautiful. I been waiting for this day. I

hate for it to be like this, but I know your pretty little ass won't cooperate." He knelt down and kissed my lips. "Don't fight me and I'll spare your life. You see, my partner wants you dead. He just mad 'cause I told him you were off limits. To him that is. Please don't make me have to have sex with a corpse. That would be so disgusting." I could tell he was smiling.

All I could do was close my eyes. I was no angel, and I know God was probably mad at me because I only prayed when I was in trouble, but please, Lord, help me! I prayed when I felt his wet mouth on my nipples. I prayed even harder when his fingers played with my pussy. I kept calling on the name on Jesus when the masked man ordered me to get up. I slowly stood up, noticing my clothes were all off. He sat down on the sofa, facing my bare ass. He glided his hand along my butt.

"I need to make all this mine! Damn, you got a fat ass!"

"Please, don't hurt me."

"No, baby, I wont hurt you. I just want to pleasure you. Let me pleasure you."

"Please," I begged.

Just then, black cap entered the room. "She tell you where the money was yet?" He looked me over. "Gotdamn, you hit that?"

"Will you give me some damn privacy?!" red cap yelled.

"Not till she tell me where the fuckin' money is. I swear I'll kill her!"

"Wait," I yelled out. "He use to go to the basement a lot. He could've hidden it anywhere down there."

Red cap stood up and grabbed my arm. "Let's check it out."

He held onto my arm tight as I guided them both downstairs. When we got down to the basement, black cap searched around quickly, breaking and throwing things. Red cap held onto me as and he searched around.

Black cap yelled out, "I got something." He removed removing stone bricks out of the wall.

We walked over to where he was and watched as black cap removed all the bricks with quickness. He found a large safe. He then pulled out a gun and aimed at the locked safe. He shot repeatedly until he was out of rounds. He tucked his gun away and flipped open the safe. It revealed lots of jewelry and I wanted to faint. I never saw that many jewels up close in my life.

"Yo' nigga robs everyone I see." Black cap grabbed a nearby duffel bag. He emptied out the clothes that was in there and loaded it with the jewelry.

"So where's our money?" red cap asked. "I want my muthafuckin' money!"

"We'll find it!" black cap said, still loading up the bag. "But right now, we got jewels."

I noticed a small plastic bag in the safe. Black cap opened that bag and saw a small ring box. He opened it to reveal a large, pink diamond ring. I bet that was worth some real money. Red cap let me go and he took the ring, examining it.

"Looks like he was saving this for you." Red cap slipped it in his pocket. He then started to go through the rest of the jewelry.

It was my time to make a run for it. I picked up a pipe and hit red hat my hardest. That got black hat's attention, and that's when I clobbered him in the stomach, making him drop the bag. I took off running like a wolf chasing its prey. I never looked back, I just ran. When I got to the top of the steps, I felt my leg being grabbed. I turned and saw one of the guys, but I didn't know which one he was. Although he still had on the ski mask the cap was gone. I was kicking at him, but it was no use. He pulled me down to him and then grabbed my neck. I tried pulling his mask off but it was too late. He had his .45 caliber in his hand and ready to kill me. I froze when he put that gun to my head.

"That's what I thought. Now get yo' ass upstairs. Imma tear yo' pussy up! You don't know who you done fucked with."

It was red hat and he was madder than ever. He forced me upstairs and soon as we got into the living room, he slapped me in my face. I fell to the floor and stayed there. He got on top of me and I struggled. Gun or not, I struggled. I felt he was going to kill me anyway so I'd go out fighting. But God was with me.

Soon as I felt him inside me, I thought my life was over. He was raping me, and there was nothing I could do about it. His partner ran into the room fast and yanked him off of me.

"Let's go," he yelled. "She making too much noise, and them shots probably attracted a lot of attention."

"That's your fault," he said as he raised up off of me.

He looked down at me and spit. "Fuck you! I'll be back to finish you off, and when I do, Imma tear yo' pussy up for real."

They both left me lying on that floor, feeling disgusted and nasty. Even though he violated me, I thanked God. He spared me again!

Chapter Seventeen

Tony looked like he wanted to give me a hug. Nobody knew about this. Not my mom, not the girls, not even Caddy. I couldn't believe I told Tony.

"I'm sorry you had to go through all of that." He rubbed my thigh.

"I think the guy that called was one of them."

"As long as you're with me, I promise I'll protect you. That's my word."

"Ever since that phone call, I been scared. He said he was coming back for me, and I wouldn't doubt if he killed me. I hope they found the money. Maybe they'll leave me alone."

"Do you think Quentin had ten million dollars?"

"Quentin did a lot of sneaky shit behind my back, so who knows."

"So Quentin was into robbing people?"

"It seems that way. I been with Quentin for all them years, and wouldn't think he'd do something like that." Then I started thinking. "Maybe them guys are wrong."

"What if they're not? There's ten million out there somewhere waiting to be claimed. Maybe he buried it."

"Are you suggesting we go back and look?"

"No, but that don't sound too bad." I leaned back in the sofa and started to think. "Not yet, you need to lay low until we found out who's following you."

I looked over at Tony and couldn't believe I told him my story. Tony was sweet and such a good friend, but at the moment, he was looking delicious.

"Hey, what about my private dance?" I asked him.

He slowly stood up. "Oh you want this dance?"

"Show me what you got."

I smiled as Tony aka White Chocolate did his moves. He was really turning me on. He got butt naked for me, and at that moment I couldn't resist. I reached out and caressed his dick, working it up and down my hand. He got the hint and lay back on the sofa, pulling me on top of him. He stripped away at my clothes and soon as my breast were revealed, he lapped away at them. I quickly placed him inside of me and rode his dick to the extreme. Tony pulled me closer onto him and I threw my head back, and moaned in excitement. I winded my hips, trying to feel every inch of his dick inside me. We both achieved an orgasm together, and I collapsed on his chest. After a moment I began to get dressed. Tony came behind me massaging my shoulders.

"I'm sorry. I…"

I cut him off, turning towards him. "It's okay, I wanted it. But do you think this will ruin our friendship?"

"I won't let it." He smiled.

I kissed Tony on the cheek. "Well, I gotta go find the girls. Call me later.

I walked away from Tony, not regretting what we just did. I was happy and satisfied. I didn't want a relationship from Tony, maybe friends with benefits. I could do that, hopefully he could, too.

Chapter Eighteen

Me and Veronica were sitting at the bar. I had a Sprite and Veronica was drinking those Blue Mutherfuckers, it was a real crazy drink. That's why her ass was tore up. I was sitting there witnessing what that drink could do to you. It was nearly closing time and time for us to go.

That bitch was falling over, flirting with whoever, and talking shit. She even thought she was at work and started to strip so I had to stop her. I bet if I wasn't pregnant, my silly ass would be drinking it, too.

I was happy to see Tony coming toward us because I couldn't handle Veronica much longer. Jessica left with Lundon awhile ago. Soon as Tony came over, he picked Veronica up and slung her over his shoulder like a jacket. She went crazy and started touching all over him. Then, she began to pound on him really hard, but he didn't seem to care. He just carried her outside.

"I never seen her this drunk," Tony said to me.

"She had too many of them blue fuckers." I laughed, thinking about her episodes all night.

"You got one drunk ass friend, and one freaky as friend that left with Lundon and Davie."

"What!"

"Yeah, I heard she wanted two men to pleasure her. Davie don't care. He was getting pussy regardless.

They done it before. Yo friend gonna have one wild night, they rough."

"She is so nasty." Soon as we hit the parking lot, Tony looked around. "Oh, follow me." I began walking toward the car. "I'll drive her car."

Tony followed me, and when it was time to put her crazy ass in the car, she went crazy. She started struggling and acting a fool. She got tired of fighting him and he quickly strapped her seatbelt in.

"I'll follow you guys," he said, walking away.

"You don't have to."

"I insist."

No need arguing with him. He was going to do it regardless. Soon as the car started moving, Veronica fell right to sleep. All the shit she done did, I bet she was tired.

When we got home, Tony did everything. He carried her upstairs to her room, took her shoes off, and tucked her in. When he was finished, I walked Tony outside to his car. Once we got there, he leaned up against it, and took me into his arms. I knew we had sex earlier, but I was starting to think it was a mistake. He wanted a relationship, I just knew it. I still loved Caddy. No matter how many times he left me, I still loved him. He had my heart. I pulled away from Tony after I felt his lips on mine.

"Good night, Tony."

"So you gonna leave me now?"

"I'm sorry, Tony, but I'm tired."

I tried to leave but Tony grabbed my hand. "I love you more than Caddy will ever love you. I have never left your side. I would never do that to a woman I love. Even if this baby isn't mine, I'll still be there."

It was real nice of Tony to say that, even though I

didn't love him like he loved me. My eyes started to tear up and I felt bad. Here I had a good man in front of me, and I wouldn't even give him a chance. Before I knew it, he grabbed me again and kissed me more passionately. I couldn't resist and I kissed him back. It was so sweet, and that kiss instantly made my panties wet.

"You better go now," I said as I backed away.

"Let me stay," he begged.

"You can't. What if Caddy comes over?"

"Who gives a fuck if he comes over? Baby, he left you hanging. His dumb ass is missing out on the most beautiful person in the world. Caddy's not coming."

"Tony, please go."

"Why don't you love me like you love him?"

"I do love you." I started to cry. "I don't know, I love both of you."

"Then be with me. If the baby is mine, I don't want him taking care of it."

I started crying harder. I thought I was going to hyperventilate. "Why am I in this situation? I fuckin' hate myself for this!" I ran away from him. "Bye, Tony. It's not you, I just need some time."

I ran into the house and shut the door behind myself. My heart was torn, and the only thing I could do was run to my bedroom. I lay across my bed and cried myself to sleep.

Chapter Nineteen

My whole weekend went by real quick. I felt bad for pushing Tony away. I shouldn't have had sex with him knowing he would want to be with me even more. I couldn't face him, so I distanced myself from him all weekend. I ignored his calls and I wouldn't come out my bedroom. I bet the girls thought I was a crazy, depressed nut. Caddy was still playing games by not calling me. He was the one I was worried about. I wanted him to stop acting childish about this whole situation and be my man again. In this short amount of time that we've been together, I've fallen deeply in love with him. I didn't know what would happen if this baby was Tony's. I have strong feelings for him as well.

I heard Jessica yelling my name. I stepped out the shower and she was in my bathroom with the phone in her hand. Talk about privacy.

"Damn, momma!" She touched my belly. "You really poking out."

"Shut up.!"

She looked at my butt. "Your ass is fat, too, but in a good way."

"Who is it?" I ignored her.

"He hung up. It was your doctor. He wants you to come to the office. He says come alone."

"I hope everything's okay." I rushed passed

Jessica to put on some clothes.

I was quick at getting dressed and I asked Jessica if she wanted to go with me. Veronica even wanted to come, so she tagged along as well. I knew the doctor said come alone, but if I had bad news, I couldn't deal with this alone.

We all sat in the waiting room for about fifteen minutes before Dr. Morrison came to get me. He let the girls come and led us to his office. He sat down behind his desk and pulled out a folder. Me and the girls sat there, eager to know what was going on.

"How you doing today, Azaria?" he asked.

"I was okay until you called. I'm nervous." I rubbed my hands together. "And my palms are so sweaty."

Dr. Morrison smiled. "I know you been having some trouble between the two fathers. I may be able to solve your problem. I think this will be great news to you. Something you want to hear."

"Well give it to me."

Dr. Morrison opened up the folder and pulled out my ultrasound.

"I know you're not sure who is the father of the baby, and was hoping the conception date would help. Well, I was off by three weeks and the recent ultrasound tells me your three weeks further than what we thought."

"Three weeks?"

"Does that tell you an answer?"

I looked at Veronica and then Jessica. "Three weeks?"

Veronica leaned over and whispered in my ear. "So it is Quentin's baby?"

I looked back at the doctor. "What's my

conception date?"

He looked through the papers again. "Mid March."

"Quentin died March 8th."

"Did you have sex after he died?"

I looked up at Dr. Morrison with tears in my eyes. I loved Dr. Morrison as my doctor. I mean, you could tell this man anything. He seemed to understand. He never judged me about bringing two men to my doctor appointments. He was actually trying to help me with this situation. I had to tell him.

I started to shake my head. "My pregnancy been up and down. First I thought I was pregnant by Quentin, and then the pregnancy test said I wasn't. Then I had sex with two men and took another pregnancy test. Then, I was pregnant."

"Sometimes home pregnancy tests are wrong," Dr. Morrison replied.

"This is some crazy shit!"

"What, Azaria?" Veronica asked. "Tony won't ever leave you, no matter what."

"Yeah, girl," Jessica agreed. "He loves you a lot."

I couldn't help but cry out loud. I bet they thought I was crazy. I cried like a big baby wanting a bottle. Dr. Morrison even walked over my way to comfort me. Every time I opened my mouth to speak, no words came out.

"It's not that bad," Jessica said.

"It's worse than you think," I said, finally getting up.

After I got myself together, I stood in front of them all. I had their undivided attention.

"I moved to Cali for a reason," I started. "Remember the phone call I got awhile back. I told you guys it was the person that probably killed

Quentin, and he was coming to kill me. Before I left to come here, I was raped on that day by one of the killers. I know they are looking for me. He wants to kill me."

Dr. Morrison eased back to his chair. He seemed disrupted by the news I just delivered. I probably should've kept it to myself about this, but I didn't care.

"Well, I don't know who he is. He had a mask on and it was night time. We were mostly in the dark, but I bet it's his baby."

They were all speechless. Jessica embraced me and Veronica followed.

"I'm sorry, Azaria." Doctor Morrison said.

I smiled. "Thanks for letting me know."

"What are you going to do?" Jessica asked.

"I'll have to tell them." I turned to the doctor. "Thanks again, I appreciate the information."

"Keep your next appointment and I'll see you then."

"Thanks."

Jessica, Veronica, and I left the office. Soon as I got into the car, I cried some more.

"Don't worry, honey." Veronica put her hand on mine. "You still got me."

"And me," Jessica yelled out.

I let out more tears as Jessica rubbed my back.

"Do you know the race of this rapist?" Jessica asked.

"He was black, I saw his hands."

"Caddy don't have to know," Jessica continued. "Kick Tony to the curb and get Caddy back into your life."

"As much as I love Caddy, I can't do that to him. I just can't. Besides, I think I'm falling in love with Tony more and more each day."

"Well, we'll see which one really loves you when you tell them the truth." Veronica started to drive.

I just sunk into my seat, feeling so mad. Why was my life taking a turn for the worst? The masked guy was probably my baby's father.

Chapter Twenty

That night when Tony called I accepted. He was happy to finally hear from me. I only had one thing on my mind, and Tony was not going to be happy.

"How you feeling today?" Tony asked when I picked up the phone.

"Not too good." I took a deep breath.

"Why?" He sounded disappointed. "Is it because you're talking to me? About the other night..."

"No!" I quickly stopped him. "I'm happy you called. We just have a situation we need to talk about. I rather not do it over the phone."

"Do you want me to come over?"

"Actually, can I come over there?"

"Yes."

"I'll be there in a minute."

I hung up the phone and rolled out the bed. I took a five minute shower and then threw on a white t-shirt and some gray capris. It was mid-August, the hottest month of the year, but for some reason it was cool today. I wasn't complaining. I needed this day.

Tony was standing outside when I pulled up. He was the perfect gentlemen, except for the temper he had awhile back. He's been sweet recently though. Hopefully after I tell him the bad news, he doesn't go crazy on me.

He reached out to me and we hugged. He kissed

my forehead and then looked at me.

"What's going on?" he asked.

"Let's go inside."

Tony wrapped his arm around me and guided me inside his apartment. It smelled so good and looked tidy. I bet he did a quick clean-up and sprayed some air freshener.

I sat down on Tony's sofa, the same sofa we fucked on. Then the thought came to my head, what if he had another woman over here before me? Maybe that's why he straightened up, to cover up her scent. Or maybe not. I better quit thinking so negative about men, at least this man. But who cares, me and Tony are just friends. So why worry?

"Are you thirsty?" he asked me.

"Water, please."

I got up and followed Tony into the kitchen. I watched as he went into the refrigerator and pulled out a bottle of Aquafina water. He handed it to me and watched me open it. I took two small sips and sat myself at his kitchen table. He sat across from me and pulled out an orange from the fruit basket off the table. He watched me and peeled his orange at the same time. He was waiting for me to talk.

"I don't know where to start," I admitted.

"Start from the beginning. We have all night."

"I told you the beginning." I sighed. "We talked about it the other night."

"Oh." He nodded. "There's more?"

"The doctor corrected me on my due date today." I began to cry. "He was off by three weeks. My conception date is more around the time that guy raped me."

He slammed the orange down. "You can't be

serious!"

"I wish I would've known. I didn't mean to get you and Caddy involved."

"Are you sure about this?"

"Dr. Morrison confirmed it."

Tony pounded his fist into the table, frightening me a second time. He saw that it startled me and he got up. He walked over to my side, knelt down and grabbed both my hands.

"I'm sorry. So there's no possibility that this baby is mine?"

"I highly doubt it. It's that guy's. Possibly Quentin's, but I'm sure it's that guy."

"At least that counts Caddy out. Did you tell him?"

"No, but I will."

"Zaria, you can count on me. I'll be your baby's father."

Tony stood up, still holding onto my hand. He took me into his arms and we hugged. He was a good man. I was so blind. He may have a temper problem, but Tony had a good heart. At that moment, I wanted to make love to Tony. I kissed his lips and he picked me up. He took me into his bedroom and handled my body so lovely. I truly was in love as he made love to me like no other man. After our lovemaking moment, he fell asleep holding onto my body. His hand lay across my belly, feeling my precious baby kick. I lay there crying silently. I missed Caddy and I wanted him back. This wasn't fair to Tony.

Chapter Twenty-One

Caddy had practically disappeared on me. No one had seen or heard from him in months. I was due any day now and I wanted Caddy to be around. I hated myself for loving Caddy so much because I was living in Tony's house. We were actually a couple, and he treated me so good. I loved him just as much. Sometimes, I wished I could have both men. My big ass even went to work with Tony and watched him dance. My girls were usually with me so I was far from lonely. He would quick freak all the women. They were disappointed, but that still didn't stop their horny asses from sticking money down his shorts.

Veronica picked up more hours at her club, at least that's what she was saying. I personally thought she finally had a friend. I didn't know why she liked to keep him a secret, but she did. Veronica has never been this secretive before.

I was finally going to meet Tony's parents. It was the beginning of November, and they were having a party for their 40th wedding anniversary. I was afraid to meet them. With me being black and the stories he told me about them, I had no business going. It was long ago stories, but the hate had to be still in their heart. Tony even lied and said I was pregnant by him. I swear they'd hate me. His brother was bringing over his fiancé, so maybe I wouldn't feel so bad. I heard she was black, too.

Tony pulled up into a large Victorian house. There were lots of cars parked out front, which confirmed we were late. Tony was the type that liked to make grand entrances, so being late was always on purpose. I didn't want to go in, but I wasn't going to leave Tony hanging. Besides, I had to show off my beautiful fitted dress which Trixsy made for me. You would've thought I paid $5000 for it. She had me looking good. It was an off the shoulder, black and red satin dress. Tony bought me a beautiful diamond necklace with matching earrings. I was looking expensive, but felt like a scared little girl.

Soon as we walked into the house all eyes were on us. Tony hadn't seen his family since he became a stripper two years ago. They talked on the phone, but he had quit coming around because of the criticism. I was glad he was finally coming around because I missed my family more than anything and wish I could go back.

"Bro," we heard a voice yell out.

I looked to my right and spotted a tall, white guy walking our way. He was just as handsome as Tony. It had to be Tony's brother, Allen, because I saw the resemblance. Following behind him was a tall, model-like black woman. She was dark-skinned, but had the most beautiful complexion. Her long, jet black hair flowed down to her ass. Someone put some really good weave in her hair, or she had some Indian in her family.

I watched as Tony and Allen embraced each other. They were so excited to see each other, they forgot about us two women standing there.

"So who's the sexy momma?" Allen asked as he

kissed my hand.

“This is my beautiful girlfriend, Azaria,” Tony rubbed my belly, “and our unborn baby.”

“You didn’t tell me you were expecting?”

“I could never find your ass.”

Allen’s woman friend, or fiancé, tried to make herself noticeable by clearing her throat. Allen grabbed her by her tiny waist and pulled her close to him.

“Sorry, baby.” He kissed her and looked our way “This is my beautiful fiancé, Catrice.”

Tony grabbed Catrice’s hand and kissed it. She then gave me some funky ass look as if I was to get jealous. He was a real gentlemen, but Catrice liked it way too much.

“Nice to meet the woman that’s making my brother happy,” Tony said as he grabbed my hand.

“You and Allen resemble a lot.” She was blushing, then she looked at me. “You’re a very lucky woman. Tony’s very handsome.”

“Yes, I am,” I said with a little sass in my voice.

“I need to steal your man for a quick second,” Allen said to me as he grabbed Tony by the shoulders. They walked away, leaving me to stand with this bitch. I wasn’t going for it, so I tried to wander away. What did she do? She followed me!

“We might as well stick together,” she said as she eased to the side of me.

“And talk about what?” I rolled my eyes. “I don’t know you.”

“Damn, your hormones are sure kicking in.”

I stopped and looked at her perfect body, and then her face. “It’s not my hormones, honey. I just don’t want to talk.”

"Awww," she teased. "Are you mad at the great connection I had with your boyfriend?"

"What connection? You were practically flirting with my man. You have your own damn man that's actually his brother," then I lowered my voice, "so what the fuck you think you and Tony have a connection for?"

"'Cause we do." She slid her hands over her hips. "Look at me, who wouldn't want me? Then look at you, you're pregnant and fat." She laughed.

So now this stuck on herself bitch has gone too far. I knew it was something about her. First she flirts with my man, then she insults me. I just wanted to smack the shit out of her, but I had to keep my cool. I didn't want to embarrass Tony, but I didn't want to look like a punk and not do shit about what she just said. I had to do something. I gave her a deadly look and walked away. I walked right into a waiter who was carrying a tray of red wine. I grabbed two glasses and walked back over to Catrice.

"You call me fat," I said as I stepped back over to her. She turned and looked at me. "But you're the bitch with red wine all over your white dress."

At that, I threw both glasses all over her and her dress. Then, I yelled sorry loud enough so everyone could hear. I wanted them all to look her way. She called me every name in the book when I embarrassed her ass. Everyone came over our way, but they catered to the clumsy, pregnant woman. One lady even yelled at Catrice for running into my drinks.

"I was only getting my boyfriend and his brother something to drink," I lied. "I didn't see her."

"It's okay, sweetheart," a nice, older lady said. "Are you okay?"

"Yes, I'm fine. Thank you."

Then she looked at Catrice. "Leave her alone, she said sorry! You probably deserved it."

Catrice made such a commotion, Tony and Allen ran back over to us.

"Baby, what happened?" Allen asked Catrice.

"Nothing," she yelled as she walked away. "Where's the bathroom?"

Allen turned toward me. "Are you alright?"

"I'm sorry, Allen." I tried to look sincere. "I guess I tripped over something."

"As long as you're okay."

Catrice walked back over and pulled Allen away from us.

"C'mon, Allen," she said.

"I'll be back," Allen yelled out to us as he was being dragged away.

We watched as Allen yanked away from her as they exchanged a few words, and she walked away and he chased after her like a lost puppy. I just shook my head in disgrace.

"I hate her," I whispered loud enough for Tony to hear.

Tony laughed. "I knew you threw that wine on purpose."

"She had it coming. She was trying to fuck with my man."

"Oh I see." He pulled me into his arms and lightly kissed my lips. "You look so good right now. I just want to eat you up."

I purred. "I bet you do."

I wrapped my arms around his waist and my belly rested below his belt. I kissed him again and rested my head on his shoulder.

"Baby," he said.

"Yes?"

"I want you to marry me."

I let go of Tony and looked into his crystal blue eyes. He was always mentioning it, but this time was different, he was serious. I stood there looking into his eyes. Why was he asking me here? I wanted to cry. Was I suppose to answer right now? My eyes started to water and before I could answer I heard someone call out Tony's name. We both looked around and saw a smiling, white couple. I knew they were Tony's parents but they didn't look that old, they actually looked good. He looked just like his dad. The woman gave Tony a hug and she held on for dear life. The man joined in hugging them both.

"I'm so happy you came, son," his father announced.

"And you got so big and strong." His mother started feeling his muscles.

"It hasn't been that long," Tony said.

"A little over a year," his mom scolded.

His father looked my way and smiled. "So is she the mother of my grand daughter?"

"Yes, this is Azaria," Tony told them. "Azaria, these are my parents, Nancy and George."

I extended my hand out to both of them. "Nice to meet you guys."

Nancy ignored my hand and gave me a hug, that was even better. George gave me a hug next and then he slightly patted my belly.

"My son sure knows how to pick a woman," George said.

I couldn't believe how nice they were. I thought they didn't like black people. I guess people did change. I turned my head, trying not to show my rosy glow from me blushing so hard. Thank God they were cool, at least for now until I pissed them off, then they'd call me every racist name in the book. Let's not hope we ever got to that.

"So, Azoe," Nancy started.

"Mom, her name's Azaria," Tony corrected.

She waved Tony away. "Anyway, Azaria, what am I going to have, a grandson or granddaughter?"

"A girl." I smiled.

"Good, Allen already gave us two grandsons."

"I have a name for her," his dad announced.

"It's alright, dad, we do have a name," Tony told him.

"What is it?"

"A surprise."

Tony grabbed my hand and hugged both his parents.

"Sorry, mom, dad, but we really have to go."

"But you guys just got here," Nancy complained.

"Azaria's tired." He lied. "We'll keep in touch."

"Good. I don't want to see strangers anymore." She kissed Tony. "I really miss you, and Azaria's family now, you and her are welcome anytime."

"Alright, mom. I'll keep in touch. Tell Allen to call me." Tony rushed me out quickly. Soon as we got outside he turned to me. "I had to get you out before they started some shit," he confessed. "Sooner or later, one of them would've said a remark that would have offended you."

"They were nice."

"They would fool you later." He started to kiss me. "Besides, I wanted to get your sexy ass home as soon as possible. You look good."

"Baby, I'm fat."

"You're not fat, you're pregnant, and you look good to be pregnant."

Tony walked me to the car and soon as we got there he began to kiss me. When I got into the kiss, it was on. I was feeling just as freaky as he was. He even pulled up my dress and tried to find my pussy under my basketball belly. When his fingers slipped in, I stopped him.

"Not here, baby," I said. "Not in front of your parents' house."

"So!" He looked around. "Nobody's watching."

He kept trying to play with my pussy. When his fingers glided in, I stopped resisting. It felt so good and I moaned as we kissed. Tony managed to hold my leg up as he continued to play in my treasure.

"Damn, baby," he nibbled on my ear, "you real wet down there. Your shit is trickling down."

When he said that I realized liquid was going down my thighs and it was a lot. "I think my water just broke!" I yelled out.

"Are you serious?"

I looked down. "Yes."

"Did I do it?"

"I don't know. Maybe the baby is ready."

Tony began to panic. After he opened the passenger door, he helped me in. He ran to the driver side and sped off. We were on our way to the hospital.

Chapter Twenty-Two

It was 1:45pm the next day when her head finally came out. I heard Veronica yelling out she had lots of hair. Trixsy fainted, she acted like she never saw a baby being born and the girl had eight nieces and nephews. Jessica was a good coach for me, thank God for her. Now Tony, he was ready, he couldn't wait to see the baby. I guess a part of him still thought the baby could be his.

I heard her crying and it brought tears to my eyes. She was so beautiful and I named her Mahalia Quentina Devro. Quentina after Quentin and I gave her my last name. Mahalia was white but I knew her skin color was going to be a darker shade. Tony swore Mahalia was his. I explained to him that most black babies came out white. My great great grandma was white, so she could have light skin because of my background. She'd probably be a honey brown color, not too dark and not too light. She had so much jet black hair. She was a little thick baby weighing 7 pounds and 4 ounces. I loved her so much.

I fell asleep after breast feeding, which went well. The nurses put her back in the nursery so I could rest and Tony went home to change. The girls left for awhile, too. I was at peace at last. I might've slept a good three hours before I heard arguing that woke me up. Tony was sitting in a rocking chair next to me and

Caddy stood on the other side of me, looking gorgeous than ever. He sported a black, leather biker jacket, and wore a crisp pair of blue jeans. He argued with Tony, telling him he had the right to be there. Caddy dogged me, and I couldn't believe he showed up.

"Why are you here, Caddy?" I asked him.

"I came to see my baby." He smiled at me. Then, he pointed to the table with a vase filled with pink roses. "Those are for you."

"She wasn't your baby back then," Tony interrupted, "so get out!"

"The baby is black! She's mine."

"She half white, so get the fuck out!"

"You get the fuck out! Yo' job is over. I'm here now."

"Just go, Caddy!" I yelled to him. "We don't want you here."

Caddy kneeled down by my bed side and pulled a small box out of his pocket. He sat it on top of my chest.

"I'm sorry I left you. I was confused, baby. I had to handle a lot of business, but we gonna be okay now. I'm ready to become a family. I only left for you. Now I want you to be my wife."

I closed my eyes, fighting back tears. "Why, Caddy? Why are you doing this to me?"

"I couldn't take that shit. I mean, Tony always being there."

"While you were gone, Tony was always there. Day and night, he never left me, no matter what!"

"Please, Zaria, can we just start all over? I was so confused."

"Confused my ass!" I folded my arms across my chest. "It's time for you to go!"

"I'm not leaving." Caddy stood his ground. "That's my baby."

I sighed and thought about the truth. I never told Caddy what was going on. I guess he had the right to know.

"My baby's name is Mahalia Quentina Devro. Mahalia might be Quentin's. Not yours, and definitely not Tony's."

"So she's some dead guy's baby?" Caddy looked angry. "What the fuck, Azaria? Did you know?"

"He died three or four weeks before I met you. The doctor had my conception date wrong."

"Wrong?" He shook his head. "She still could be mine. The doctor could be wrong about your date."

"She's not yours!"

"You knew you were pregnant when you met me, huh?" He started to get loud. "You was probably trying to trick me until captain white boy saved you. You was looking for a baby daddy."

"No, Caddy. I didn't know I was pregnant."

"Yeah right. All you bitches are the same."

"You're fuckin' lucky I can't get out this bed," I yelled.

Tony stepped up. "If she has to tell you to leave again, I'll kick your ass out this hospital myself."

Caddy laughed, then turned to me, not paying Tony any attention. "I actually fell in love with you and you did me so dirty."

I was crying. "It's not even like that. It was never like that."

"That hurts."

Caddy turned around to leave, pushing Tony out his way. I put my head down and cried some more. Tony sat on the edge of the bed. He eased toward me and took me into his arms. He let me cry on his chest.

"He don't mean none of that shit," Tony said. "He just wanted to get the heat off of him. Don't pay no attention to his bitch ass. I still love you."

"I'm so sorry, Tony." I sniffled.

"For what?"

"Getting you into this."

"Don't even worry, baby. All we do now is look to the future." Tony kissed my tears away.

Chapter Twenty-Three

Three months had gone by and Mahalia was getting big. I lost all my weight and maybe more. Stress was killing me and my life was getting harder.

I contacted Quentin's parents to get a blood test to find out if Mahalia was his. My heart broke when the tests came back negative. Quentin was not her daddy, which left the masked, red hat wearing rapist.

Then, Tony started to stress me out because he wanted a paternity test, too. He swore she was his. I knew she wasn't because she was a little darker than an average biracial child. Tony said he had Indian blood in him and that's why she was dark. He was making up everything for this child to be his. So I went and got it done, 0%, of course. He couldn't handle it and he flipped out like he just knew she was his child. I had to hear about it everyday, like I cheated on him. He threw it in my face about not being the father. He even said 'fuck me and the neighborhood's baby.' Oh that was the last straw. I couldn't take that verbal abuse much longer, so I left his ass and moved back in with my girls.

They loved having a baby in the house. We all were taking care of Mahalia so she had a mom and three great aunties. I started looking for a job. My money was running low and I had no man to support us. Veronica was trying to get me a job at the strip club but hell no, I couldn't do that shit. I was a mother and would never stoop that low. No offense to the women like Veronica that loved it, it just wasn't me.

I finally got a job at a very expensive women's store in the mall. It was okay money. Not much, but I was going to survive. I even met a new friend name Chari who was really cool. I related to her because she was a single mom. Chari was very wild though, she reminded me of Jessica. They acted the same, dressed the same, and their body resembled. Well, except Chari's tits were real. She was a very pretty woman. She had long, wavy, jet black hair that fell a little past her shoulders. Her light skin was very fair, which took after her mother's side of the family. Chari and I became best friends, and it seemed as if I had known her forever.

Chari had a son name Reginald Jr. She named him after his father who left her for another woman. Now that Chari lost all her weight, and look better than ever, Reginald was trying his hardest to get her back. She wasn't even thinking about his old, played out ass. She was too busy trying living the single life. I made the biggest mistake when I took Chari out with my roommates. Never again! Her and Jessica ass got into it all night long, and over some niggas. They were everywhere, but it seemed as if those two were loving the same ones. One man, Jay, seemed to be the finest with phat pockets, so you know them freaks/gold diggers were after him. Even Trixsy was trying to take him home. Unfortunately, Trixsy backed off when he was about sex only. She wasn't a freak like the other two.

It was Saturday afternoon and we were very busy in the store. I wasn't concerned about the customers, my dumb ass was in the back arguing with Tony. He called me with some bullshit about coming to get Mahalia tonight. What was wrong with him? He wasn't her daddy, and since we broke up, he quit coming around. So why now?

"Last month it was over between us and you quit calling. You quit thinking about Mahalia. So why the fuck you calling my phone now?"

"I promised I would always be there for you and her," he stated.

"No you didn't! You said, 'fuck me and the neighborhood's baby.' Remember those words?"

I could hear him sigh. "I still love you and I definitely love Mahalia. I just went crazy when I found out she wasn't Quentin's or mine. I thought if she was Caddy's you'd leave me."

"Caddy is not her dad neither. I told you what happened."

"Zaria, really look at her." Tony sounded depressed. "As much as I hate to say it, she looks just like Caddy. Every time I look at her, I see him."

"And if she happens to be his, you were still s'pose to be by my side. You always said you'd never leave me. I'm working, and taking care of my baby by myself. I don't need no man, so don't ever call me no more."

I quickly flipped my phone shut and let out a small scream. I was not going to let Tony ruin my day. Right before I left the back room, my phone rang again. I looked at the caller ID and saw it was Tony again. I threw the phone in my purse and set it back on the desk. I put on my fake ass smile so I could deal with those high maintenance women that came to the store.

I opened the door and walked right back into the scene. I watched the manager, Vicki, look around the store. I bet she was looking for me. Vicki was Miss Super Fly, so she thought. She was beautiful indeed. She was a skinny, red headed, classy woman who had no business working. Her husband was the top dog at C&V, which was the law firm Jessica worked at. Jessica slept with Vicki's husband plenty of times to get what she wanted. He was crazy over Jessica, he seemed as if he loved her as much as he loved his wife. What did that girl do to those men?

Vicki spotted me and walked up swinging her long, bouncy red hair.

"I don't like helping customers," she said with an attitude. "I had to do your job while you were off hiding somewhere."

I rolled my eyes. "Vicki, please. I was just talking to Tony. It didn't take long."

She smiled. "White Chocolate?"

"Yeah."

"You get back with him?" She sounded disgusted.

"No, we were just talking."

She hated the fact that Tony was my boyfriend. He was so hot, and sexy, but his ass was a no good, lying dog!

"Anyway," she put her hand on her hips and pointed, "you need to help that couple over there."

I looked over in the direction of the evening wear. There was a black couple and they had their backs turned. They looked easy to sell to. The guy looked good from the back, wearing a pair of baggy jeans and a yellow polo shirt. He looked very decent. The young lady looked ghetto though. Her big, apple ass was squeezed into the tightest jeans ever. Then she had on a tight belly shirt that displayed a big dragon tattoo right above her ass. I rolled my eyes at Vicki, then I put my fake ass smile. I strolled over to the happy couple.

"Can I help you guys today?" I asked.

Soon as they turned around my smile disappeared. In front of me stood the last man I thought I'd ever run into. Why was this shit happening to me? Why did I have to see him? Although I hated him, I could feel my panties getting wet because his ass was looking good.

"Zaria?" Caddy seemed happy to see me.

"Hello, Caddy," I said dryly. I smiled at the woman.

"How are you doing?"

I frowned a little. "I'm okay."

"You look real good."

"Caddy," the woman called out, "aren't you going to introduce me?"

"Hold on," he told her. "I was gettin' there."

Caddy turned his attention back to me. "Azaria, this is Eve." He looked back at her. "Azaria and I use to date."

"Date?" she repeated.

"She's also my baby mama," he said proudly.

"What!" Her ghetto voice was loud. "You didn't tell me you had a baby. Yo' ass was trippin' 'cause I got three."

I was shocked my damn self at Caddy admitting he fathered my baby. What the hell was wrong with him and Tony? They playing games with me and my baby. They were confused and I was tired of it. My head was going to be all fucked up over this. Eve was real pissed though. She rolled her neck at Caddy and had her hands on her hips. She was waiting for him to respond, but his attention was on me.

"Your baby?" I questioned him.

"Yeah." He was smiling like he was a proud father.

"So now you want to claim my baby?"

"Zaria, quit trippin'. Imma be there for my little angel."

Caddy pulled out a wad of cash and started flipping through his money. Eve's attitude went away quick and her eyes got big. She had the biggest grin on her face. He peeled off ten hundred dollar bills and handed them it to me. My money was low and I needed it bad, but I just stared at it. Eve's hands went right back on her hips, and she looked at me like I should've took it.

"Take it, Zaria," Caddy said as he tried to shove the money in my hand. I yanked my hand away. "You don't have to like me. I just want to be there for my baby."

Before I could speak, Eve stepped in front of him, blocking me. I swear if I wasn't at work I'd kick her ghetto ass.

"You leaving me for her or what?" She rolled her neck.

He pushed Eve to the side. "If she'll take me back."

"You fuckin' foul!" Eve yelled. "I'll find me another baller, I'm out!"

Caddy ignored Eve. He looked at me waiting for an answer. Eve interrupted again and held her hand out.

"I need money for a cab. You can't leave me stranded, and you messed my hair do up last night.

You owe me $600 for that."

"Hitch a ride and fuck your hairdo," Caddy told her.

She hissed and stormed off. He did her so wrong.

He grabbed me and pulled me into his arms. He stuffed the money in my Chanel suit jacket. I was mad at myself for giving in, but I loved Caddy, and I was happy he was holding me at this moment. I would never let this man go, baby daddy or not.

Chapter Twenty-Four

Soon as I stepped into the house with Caddy by my side, the girls frowned at me. I knew they'd be pissed. Even when he said what's up, they gave him attitude back. I knew it was going to happen. Caddy left me with no real explanation, and I was the dumb ass to run right back into his arms. I guess I really loved him.

Veronica walked up to me and pulled me by the arm. "C'mon, girl."

She pulled me into the kitchen with Jessica, following. Trixsy stayed in the living room still holding Mahalia. I bet she was going to get on Caddy. I plopped down on the stool. I wasn't looking forward to what was next but my girls were only looking out for me.

"What the hell is wrong with you?" Veronica yelled at me. "Bringing his ass back into your life will not make you happy. All he's going to do is leave you again."

Jessica smiled. "He do look good, girl. I'd probably take his ass back, too."

"Jessica, you're not helping." Veronica slapped Jessica's arm, then she looked at me. "Why'd you take him back?"

"I don't know." I put my head down on the

counter and then looked back up. "I guess I love him."

"Who don't you love? You were just with Tony claiming he was the love of your life."

"Tony don't know what he wants. I was only with Tony 'cause Caddy was gone."

"You mean to tell me you don't have no love for Tony?"

"Not really."

"Bullshit!" Veronica wasn't buying it.

"Okay, I have a little love, but I've always loved Caddy more."

Veronica just shook her head. "So what's his damn excuse?"

"Tony," I blurted out. "I mean who could blame Caddy for leaving me, I had Tony in our relationship."

"Do you think Caddy will take care of another man's baby?"

"Yes." I was confident. "The other man wasn't in my life, so he don't have to worry about some other man taking over."

"Did you guys ever get a paternity test?" Jessica interrupted. "Mahalia does favor Caddy. You never know."

"Jessica, you know damn well Caddy's not that baby's daddy," Veronica snapped. "Dr. Morrison was right the last time. The ultrasound don't lie." I just shrugged my shoulders. "Fine," Veronica continued. "Just take a damn blood test."

"No!" I exclaimed. "If Caddy don't want one, then we're good."

"I agree." Jessica looked at Veronica. "Just leave them alone."

"I'm just looking out for her. I hate seeing her lock herself in that damn bedroom and cry her eyes out. She's been through too much."

I stood up from the stool. "Thank you, Veronica, for looking out for me, but I'll be fine."

I walked out of the kitchen and back into the living room. Caddy was rocking Mahalia in the rocking chair. Trixsy was sitting on the sofa reading a hair magazine. Caddy looked up from the baby and smiled at me.

"She so beautiful," Caddy said.

"I know." I walked over to him. "She looks like her mama, huh?"

"Yeah, she looks like her mama alright. The most prettiest girls in the world." He looked back at her. "She really does look like me. Don't you think?"

I stared at my baby and smiled. I saw my precious baby every day and never thought about her looking like Caddy. I didn't want to get my hopes up, but she did look like him. They do say babies will look like whoever you want them to look like.

Caddy kissed my lips and I smiled. "I never intended to hurt you. I should've been a man and stood by your side. I can't take back the past, but I will promise you a good future if you let me."

Trixsy looked up from the magazine. "Awww, so sweet."

I kissed him again and threw my arms around him. I didn't care what Veronica said about Caddy, I loved him. I love this man. Just then, Jessica and Veronica stood in the doorway and Jessica was smiling her ass off.

"All I got to say is you better do my girl right." Jessica walked over and slapped Caddy on the arm. "I'll come beat your ass if you don't."

"Yeah." Caddy cracked a smile. "I bet your freaky

ass would love to beat my ass."

She laughed. "With Zaria's permission."

"You're so crazy, Jessica." I laughed along with them.

"Gurl, I'm just keepin' it real."

"I bet you are."

We laughed for awhile, then the room fell silent. We all looked Veronica's way, who was still standing in the doorway. She didn't look happy, she stood there looking evil as ever. Caddy stood up and put the baby in the bassinet.

"Well, I better be on my way." He stretched his arms and walked back over to me. He kissed me on the lips, using a little tongue. Not too much because we had an audience watching. "I'll pick you up in a couple of hours," he told me.

"Okay."

He waved to the girls as he walked to the door. "You women have a nice day."

"Alright then, Caddy," Trixsy yelled out.

"You have a nice day, too," Jessica added.

Caddy looked Veronica's way. "I love you, too, Veronica."

"Yeah whatever." She rolled her eyes.

Caddy didn't give up. I guess he wanted Veronica to fully accept him. He walked up to her and unfolded her arms.

"Veronica, don't you trust me with your friend?" He looked her in her frowning face. "I love her so much. I love Mahalia, and I know she's mine. She's my world. Her and Azaria."

Veronica put her finger in Caddy's face. "I swear, Caddy, if you fuck up, Imma seriously kick your ass."

She rolled her eyes one last time and smiled at him. It was fake, but at least she was trying. Veronica was my girl. I was kinda glad she was defensive over me.

Chapter Twenty-Five

Caddy came back later that evening as promised and he was dressed to impress in some black jeans and a black white t-shirt. Jessica canceled her plans for the evening to baby-sit.

Veronica had a date. Lately, she had been meeting men on Blackplanet.com. She was pretty close to being the next Jessica because the girl had a different date every week. She claimed the site was addictive and she couldn't stop flirting with men and meeting them. We told her about meeting men on the internet, it was so dangerous. I hoped she never ran into a maniac. The mystery man tonight was Lenny. His screen name was slangin_big_ones, what a pervert!

Trixsy stayed home but had company in her room. He was a regular, the guy Roger that was her fiancé. She had calmed down and says she might settle with him. They were always together and he was so nice to her. I was happy for her.

Caddy took me out to a small bar, nothing fancy since we both just wanted a little drink. It was about 8:30, and there were a few regulars hangin' around the bar. Most of them were trying to bum off Caddy, but he cussed the whole damn bar out and they left him alone. We sat at the bar and he ordered Absolute vodka with orange juice and I ordered a cosmopolitan. We started drinking and Caddy put his hand on my thigh, which was covered with my tight fitting Seven jeans.

"All these niggas staring at you, we might have to go." Caddy kept looking around. "But it's all good. You are so beautiful."

I blushed. "Thank you."

"I won't go nowhere. I have no reason to."

"You better not!" I grabbed his chin and pulled him in for a kiss. "'Cause I missed you so much."

"All I was doing was thinking about you."

"So who was the woman you brought into the store?"

"Eve, I met her a couple of weeks ago."

"And you was taking her shopping already?"

Caddy smiled. "She needed a dress for her brother's wedding and I told her I'd buy it. Besides, she deserved it."

"What do you mean she deserved it?"

"She was nice to me."

"So you really did fuck that hoe?"

"Okay." He laughed. "I fucked her."

"With a condom?"

"Of course!"

I rolled my eyes. "How come we didn't use one?"

"What is this question leading to?"

"Why, Caddy?"

"I didn't have one, and I wanted you so bad." I shook my head. "Of course, I was loving the way your pussy felt. I thought I was having sex with a goddess."

"Yeah I bet." I slapped his thigh.

Caddy grabbed my hand and massaged it. He stared into my eyes and I stared into his beautiful brown eyes. I really did see Mahalia in him, or was I just imagining it?

"For real, you are my goddess. Besides beautiful, you're perfect in every way. I really fucked up. I was so selfish and I'm sorry."

"I know. You don't have to keep apologizing."

"I'll apologize to you all night."

"What you doing in California, man," we heard a voice yell.

We both turned around to see a tall, black man with a wild ass beard. Soon as Caddy saw him, he wasn't happy.

"Yo', James, been looking all over for you, and..." Soon as he noticed me he stopped. "Oh sorry, Caddy. I didn't realize the young lady sitting next to you."

Caddy gave him a look that said, 'Get the fuck outta here.' The guy quickly turned around and walked away. Who was he and why did he feared Caddy like that?

"What was that about, baby?" I asked.

"Some crazy, old friend."

"So you're not from California? I thought you lived here your whole life."

"I was gone for awhile, but now I'm back. Most people don't know, like his sorry ass." Caddy stood up. "Let's get out of here."

I sipped some more of my drink. "I was just getting tipsy."

"You can get real tipsy at my house."

I smiled. "Alright, that sounds better."

Caddy grabbed my hand led me outside, back into his car. Then, we were off to his place.

Chapter Twenty-Six

Caddy couldn't keep his hands off me in the car. Soon as we got into the house, it was on! We were both naked in the living room, clothes everywhere, and didn't care. I stood in the middle of the floor while Caddy sucked on my nipples. He slid his way down to my belly, lightly sucking and circling around my belly ring. I was so horny at that moment. I grabbed him up and pushed him back down on the sofa. He sat with his legs open and all ten inches stood straight up, just calling my precious inner flower to come join. I sucked on my fingers and then slipped them down in between my thighs. I moaned, as I watched Caddy moaned and lick his lips in excitement. He seemed to be loving it more than me. I would always play with myself for Quentin and he would jack off. That was his thang and I guess Caddy loved it, too, minus the jacking off.

I walked up to Caddy with my hand stroking my freshly shaved pussy, and I stood in his face. He grabbed my hand and started to suck my fingers. Then, he then immediately buried his head between my creamy thighs. I threw my head back and placed my right leg over his shoulder. He grabbed my ass, pulling me in deeper. I felt his warm, thick tongue exploring my insides and I screamed in pleasure.

It seemed like thirty minutes went by as he pleased me. He was now pumping seven of his ten inches inside of me. I was bent over and getting my ass slapped at the same time. I was reaching my climax when he started pumping faster. I knew he was ready, then he let it out inside of me. He grabbed my breast and we both fell back on the sofa. I sat on his lap trying to catch my breath. I was feeling so good right now. I loved Caddy!

I lay back on his chest and we were silently enjoying our happy moment. It was spoiled by his cell phone ringing. He reached down to his pants and took it out his pocket. I wish he would've left it alone, but Caddy was different than Tony. He was like Quentin, soon as that phone rang, they were out. When he answered it, he walked away toward the window to get privacy. I was his woman now, h he had no privacy. I heard him speak a few words, including he'd be there in twenty minutes. I was mad.

After hanging up he looked over at me. I frowned at him, hoping he'd change his mind. I knew he wasn't thinking about me, he was thinking about money. He sat on the edge of the bed.

"Baby." He tried to come in for a kiss. I quickly turned my head.

"So you just gonna leave me like that?" I pouted. "This is our first night back together and you gonna leave me?"

"I promise it won't take me long. This will be quick."

"Can't it wait? Don't you got other people to do stuff for you? I mean, what is it that you do when you just get up and go?"

"Right now I'm trying to get my life straight and me running around doing these errands is what's gonna make us set for life."

I rolled my eyes but asked no more questions. I finally gave in to him and kissed him good and long.

"Take a quick shower with me," he said as he got up.

"Okay." I followed.

* * * * * * * * * * * * * *

I jumped in the shower with Caddy, and it was in and out for him. I stayed in longer, enjoying the large shower all to myself. I practically stayed in there for ten more minutes after he left out.

I turned off the shower and wrapped in the big towel he left for me. I walked around his huge bathroom, looking for some oil or lotion. His chocolate skin was never ashy, always glistening. At least his ex-wife had to leave some good stuff somewhere.

When I couldn't find any in the bathroom, I walked into the huge bedroom. I stood in the middle of the floor scanning his room. The average person usually kept some in their bathroom or dresser. There was nothing in the bathroom and his dressers were decorated with candles and a couple of statues of naked women. Practically bare. Where did he keep his personal care stuff? I looked at the chest, his TV, the nightstands, but they were all covered with decorative things. No lotions, no oils, nothing.

Now I was just being nosy when I saw the huge

walk-in closet. Caddy had tons of clothes, shelves full of shoes, and everything was coordinated. I spotted a wooden chest just like the one in the bedroom, but it had a lock on it. He must've had something personal in there. I walked through the closet, going straight to the back and found a door. This closet was so big that it had another door. It probably led to his coats or something. I was going to walk away, but my nosy instincts told me to open that door. Maybe he hid all his wife's things in there.

Just my luck, the door was open. I was so amazed at what stood behind that door, it was beyond my imagination. It was like an office. There was a large cherry desk with a huge black leather chair sitting behind it. There were tons of book shelves, filled with books. There were file cabinets, a small sofa, a 42' flat screen TV, and a huge statue of a naked woman. Even his walls had beautiful paintings of black and white art. I wasn't the type to browse around, but this room had me curious, I mean, it was hidden behind his closet. Why didn't he have his office downstairs? When I spotted a picture of me on his desk, I was even more curious. The shocking part about the picture was it was taken two years ago. How did Caddy get a picture of me from two years ago, I never gave it to him. I shrugged that off, thinking Veronica may have slipped it to him.

I started opening drawers and the first one I opened made my jaw drop. The first thing I saw was Quentin's 'Q' platinum medallion, which he had specially made for him. Then, there was a small box next to that medallion. When I opened it, it was the same pink diamond ring that was stolen from Quentin's safe, the one that red hat man took. The same man that raped me. All kinds of thoughts flashed through my head. Was Caddy the red hat man? Did he kill Quentin? Maybe this was a coincidence. Caddy don't know nothing about that. He lived here, and we were in New York. Tears started to run down my face as I continued to search for some answers behind what I found. I was still in denial. Caddy couldn't be the Quentin's murderer and definitely not the red hat man that night. He was my lover, my everything. Then it clicked. The phone call I received. Was he warning me about Caddy? No! I needed to calm down. None of this could be true. Maybe I was dreaming, and I'd waked up real soon. I'd just leave this room and when I turn around, the door would be gone. Before I left the room, I noticed another chest behind the door. That one was just like the other two but had no lock on it. I walked over to it and slowly opened it. OHMIGOD! The chest was full of money. Possibly the millions of dollars that everyone wanted. Maybe he found Quentin's money, or whoever's money. Damn! Could this really be?

I quickly closed it and ran out that room. I ran all the way into the bedroom and into a corner. I knelt down holding my knees, and I cried. My towel fell off, exposing my naked trembling body. Did Caddy want to kill me too? Was this all a set up? I had to get out the house before he came back. I quickly got up and dressed myself. I was rushing around looking for all my shit. When I finally got everything together, I flew to the front door, and WHAM, there he was.

Chapter Twenty-Seven

Shutting the door behind himself, Caddy stood there holding a briefcase. I tried to stay calm, but the sweat developing on my forehead told it all. I knew I was really standing in front of Quentin's murderer. Caddy seemed relaxed. Actually, he had a bit of a smile on his face. Did he just get finish killing someone else? He set his briefcase on a nearby glass table.

"Did I take long?" He looked at my shoes.

"Jessica might be tired of the baby," I lied. "I was going to check on her."

"Well, let's go get her. I want her to stay over, too."

"You want me to bring her back here?"

"Yeah." He seemed confused. "I want my baby here, too."

"Your baby?"

Caddy walked closer to me and I stepped back, almost tripping over nothing. I was scared and he could tell there was something wrong with me.

"Did something happen while I was gone?" he asked.

"I was...well uh..." I stuttered. "You consider Mahalia yours?"

"I told you earlier she's mine. Why, what happened?" He looked around his house. "Did that punk ass Tony come by? How he know where the fuck I live?"

"Calm down, Caddy," I said still backing up. "Tony didn't come by."

"Then what's wrong? Why you trippin'?"

I was scared as hell. Standing in front of me was the love of my life, I loved him as much as I loved Quentin. Did this man kill him? Did he also rape and get me pregnant? But how? How did he find me?

Caddy finally got to me and he gently touched me. "C'mon, baby, let's go lay down."

I pulled away. "I gotta go!"

I started walking away fast and he caught up with me. I was almost to the door when he grabbed my arm.

"What the fuck is your problem?" he yelled at me.

"You," I yelled back.

"What did I do?"

"How'd you end up in my bedroom that night?"

"What night?"

"The night I met you at the party."

"Why you trippin' and shit?"

I hesitated. "You knew me before that night, didn't you?"

Caddy backed away from me and stared at me. He looked disappointed, he even tried to open his mouth a couple of times but nothing came out. Suddenly, he came back to me and gently grabbed my arm. He walked me into the living room. I didn't fight or anything, I just complied. Who knows what he had up his sleeve. Besides, the touch he gave me said he wasn't going to hurt me. I think he just wanted to explain himself.

"Caddy," I began.

"Please, don't say anything. Let me speak first." I slowly sat down on the sofa and he sat down next to me. “You seen my office?” he asked.

“I wasn’t snooping. I was just looking for.....”

“You don’t have to explain.” He was calm. “I’m the one that need to do some explaining.”

He seemed sad. I knew this man was evil if he killed Quentin and raped me, but a part of me still loved him. He was silent for a minute and I was crying.

“What did you do?” I asked.

“Quentin was dirty,” he began. “He was into other things. You don’t know him like I did. We were partners.”

“Partners? I never seen you or even heard of you.”

“Because it was a secret.”

“Me, Quentin, my other boy, Rahiem, and my cousin, Josh, all worked together here in Cali. That’s how I was able to find you. I knew you’d come stay with Veronica. Well, the guy that called you, I bet that was Rahiem. Quentin killed Josh. We made good money doing hits and robbing people, mostly on the West coast, but we got around. I guess Quentin got a little greedy in our last hit together and he plotted to steal all the money, which was close to twenty million dollars. Josh was at the spot when Quentin came in and killed him and stole all of the money. He thought he was smart and tried to act like somebody broke into the place and killed Josh, robbing us with all the money. Me and Rahiem watched Quentin like a hawk for a couple of weeks and that bitch Sonya gave it away by spending some serious loot. So me and Rahiem did what we had to do. We killed Sonya, too. Her house was where we finally found all the money.”

“He was with her like that?” I mumbled to

myself.

"Sonya was also a crack head. A damn good one though, her ass was still looking good. She had this dungeon looking basement, and that's where we found the money and more jewelry. I don't know where Quentin stole all the jewelry from, but trust me, he stole all of it. So yeah, baby, I killed his ass!"

"You were trying to kill me, too!"

"Naw, baby." He touched me. "I wanted you. I always wanted you. I hated Quentin's dirty ass because you loved him so much. He talked about you all the time, and I just knew you had to be mine."

"Even if you had to rape me!" I screamed. "That was you that raped me, right?"

Caddy put his head down and that answered my question. I was in love with the man that raped me. He knew Mahalia was his because he raped me. If he tracked me down, did he want to kill me, too?

"I really did leave Olivia for you," he explained. "I love you so much."

"But you raped me, and you were so brutal!"

"I'm sorry, Azaria. I wasn't in my right mind at the time. I was high and didn't know no better."

I moved away from Caddy. I got up from the sofa and looked down at him. I hacked up the biggest spit wad and it went flying on his face. He just sat there without flinching

"I gotta go!" I turned and walked away.

"What are you going to do now?" Caddy got up and followed me. What the hell did he mean? Imma get as far as I can from his crazy ass!

"Stay the fuck away from me, Caddy! I hate you!"

"You don't mean that, baby. You just mad right now."

"I do mean it!" I turned back toward him. "I hate you!"

I turned back around and tried to walk away. Caddy grabbed my arm and brought my body into his.

"I let you go before." He looked into my eyes, and I saw the evil in him. "I can't let you leave me again. I fell in love with you and I know you love me. You can't go."

Was I in trouble? Would he let me live? Should I just fight him until I was dead?

"Please, Azaria, listen to what I have to say." Caddy's hand touched mine. "I really love you. I'd do anything for you. Back then, I was on something crazy, you know. But right now, I love you to death. That's for real. I want you and Mahalia in my life, and I swear I'll go legit."

I put my head down, trying to hide my feelings from Caddy. I didn't want him to see me giving in, because I was. Why did I love this man so much? He hurt me, and I still loved him.

"You know what, Caddy," I started, "I really need to go home. I can't think right now. Just let me clear my mind."

"Can I take you out for breakfast in the morning?"

"Tell me, Caddy!" I ignored his question.

"Tell you what?"

"The story on how you ended up in my bedroom that night?"

Caddy took a deep breath. He walked away from me and around the sofa. My eyes followed his every move.

"You think I came back to rape you again?" He looked at me.

"What were you trying to do?"

"I didn't intend on having sex with you that night. I came back to get to know you. I wanted you to be my girl. Everything I told you then was true. I have no more to hide. I told you everything."

I sighed. "Just take me home."

"Azaria..."

"Can I smack the shit out of you?"

"Azaria, I..."

And then I did it, I ran up to him and I smacked him across the face. Although my hand hurt like hell, it felt good.

"Now take me home!" I walked back to the door.

Chapter Twenty-Eight

Soon as Caddy pulled up to the house, I opened the door and flew out. I didn't feel like fumbling around for my keys, so I banged on the door like I was the police. I looked back to see Caddy getting out of his car. Nobody was answering the door, so I searched through my purse and came across my keys quicker than I thought. Caddy was right behind me when I opened the door. He stood there looking like a puppy dog in love. So fuckin' pitiful! I felt bad, but I slammed the door right in his face. I quickly locked the door and leaned against it. He knocked hard and started calling my name. I knew all the banging would wake the girls. Trixsy was the first down with Jessica and Veronica following.

"What the fuck's going on?" Trixsy asked as she ran down the stairs.

I didn't say anything. I just leaned against the door crying, listening to Caddy call my name and apologize over and over.

"What happened, Zaria?" Veronica walked up to me.

"Yeah," Jessica was right behind her, "what his ass do this time?"

"What didn't he do?" I continued crying.

The girls helped me to the sofa and I lay down.

Trixsy left and came back with a blanket. Jessica screamed through the door for Caddy to go away. She threatened him by saying she'd call the cops and his dirty ass left quick. The situations he just told me, he knew he couldn't be caught by the police. Besides, he had that briefcase in his car that he brought into the house earlier. Just imagine what was in there.

The girls sat around me and waited for my story but I didn't say a word. All I did was cry.

* * * * * * * * * * * * * **

It took me awhile, but I finally told them everything. They were as shocked as I was. They couldn't believe Caddy was the one that killed Quentin. I still couldn't believe it. He was so sweet to me, and to know that the man I loved was the man that raped me was a lot. Me and the girls talked the rest of the night until Mahalia woke up. Jessica volunteered to feed her, and they all let me rest. I did what I knew best. I went upstairs to my bedroom and locked the door. I knew I had a baby out there, but I also knew she was better in their hands right now than mine. I stayed in my room for a whole day and a half. I would've stayed longer but I missed my baby. I wanted to see her smile. Maybe she could brighten my day.

Jessica was closer to Mahalia, so I went straight to her room knowing that's where my baby was. Jessica was sleep in her bed and Mahalia lay sound asleep next to her. It was 1:15 in the afternoon, Jessica must've been tired. I was mad at myself for putting Mahalia on her. I knew Jessica probably had things to do. She stayed home just to take care of my baby. All because of that damn Caddy that put me in this depression stage.

I grabbed my baby, trying not to wake Jessica, and I then tip toed out of her room and downstairs. I landed in the kitchen where Trixsy and Chari was talking. What was Chari doing here?"

"Good afternoon, girl!" Trixsy said as she sat a whole meal on the table. "Come on, honey, eat this."

"I'm not hungry," I said, looking over at Chari wondering if Trixsy told her everything.

"You haven't eaten in two days."

I kissed Mahalia. "I missed her."

"You okay?"

"I'm good," I said as I sat in front of the plate.

"That's right," Chari interrupted, "you better eat."

"What are you doing here?" I asked her. "Aren't you suppose to be at work?"

"Well, hello to you, too." She rolled her eyes.

"Sorry, hey, girl." I paused. "Trixsy tell you?"

"Yeah."

I looked at Trixsy. "Big mouth."

"Well, you never called off work." Trixsy said defensively. "Chari was wondering what the hell was going on."

I sighed. "I'm good now. All I want to do is get out of this house."

"And go where?" Trixsy asked.

"White Chocolate." I smiled.

"There's your damn problem right there, fucking two different men at the same time. You can't go back and forth from Tony to Caddy. I know I probably do it, but there's feelings involved in your situation. They both love you, girl. You cant be doing that shit."

"I can do whatever I want."

"That's why your ass always crying in that damn room. You have a daughter now, Zaria. You can't be going into your room and locking the door. Jessica couldn't do nothing for two days 'cause she had your baby."

"It's only the weekend. I knew she had to work tomorrow."

"She had plans though."

"Just shut up!" I knew she was right, but I didn't want to hear it.

I just had a real problem with those two men. I got depressed easily and tended to lock myself in my room. I knew that was a big problem. Trixsy knew it, too, so why was she making a big deal out of this shit. She needed to help me instead of yell.

"I called off work, too," Chari said. "Why don't you and the baby get dressed? We can go out somewhere."

"Sounds good, Chari. Thanks."

Trixsy stayed silent as I got up with the baby. We went upstairs to get dressed for the day.

Chapter Twenty-Nine

Me and Mahalia back to the house around 8:30 that night and I was feeling a little better. Chari took us out to lunch and we shopped for awhile. I was loving my time out, no men to think about, and that's what I needed. Soon as I got home, Tony was on my mind again. I wanted to tell him about Caddy. I knew I shouldn't be telling him, but I needed to let it out and apologize . Nothing more.

After I lay Mahalia down to sleep, I took a long, hot shower. I put on something comfortable and lay across my bed with the phone. I dialed Tony's phone number.

"Hello?" an unrecognizable woman's voice answered the phone.

"Uh...I think I have the wrong number."

"Well, who are you looking?"

"Tony."

"He's right here. Hold on."

I was about to hang up. I couldn't believe a woman answered his phone. Okay, well maybe he had a long lost sister that he never told me about. Maybe she was a cousin staying with him.

"Yeah?" he answered, sounding sexy as ever.

"Tony?"

"Yeah?"

"Uh, is this a bad time?"

"Azaria?"

"Yes."

"Naw, what's wrong?"

"I just wanted to talk."

He sighed. "So now you want to talk to me?"

"I'm sorry about the other day. I just..."

"Sorry, Zaria, I gotta go."

I was mad at the way he was doing me. "But, Tony..."

"I don't want to disrespect you right now. You really don't want to hear this."

"Hear what?"

"Me getting my dick sucked."

I quickly hung up the phone, the nerve of that ass hole. He sure did find him a girl quick. I thought his sorry ass was over there missing me. Damn, I hate men, I hate em' all!

* * * * * * * * * * * * * *

The next morning Mahalia woke up at eight. I got up with her and took her downstairs to fix her a bottle. Jessica was in a pink and white pant suit drinking coffee. She had her briefcase on the counter and was ready for work. The same thing I should be doing. I bet I was fired by now, so why even bother. Maybe I should go out and find a new job.

"Are you feeling better, sunshine?" Jessica asked as she took a sip of her coffee.

"Somewhat."

"You going to work?"

"I'll try, if Veronica will babysit."

"Girl, you know she will, go on and get ready. Working might take that stress off."

"Yeah, you right."

I walked up to Jessica and gave her a hug with one arm, while the other held Mahalia. I knew Jessica needed more than a hug. She did everything for me and my baby and she never complained once about babysitting. It was like she knew what I was going through. It was hard always telling them my problems, they didn't know how it felt to be me. I was in love with a murderer and a male whore. The bad thing was, I still wanted both.

"Maybe tonight I'll cook dinner for everyone." Jessica smiled at me. "We can all sit and talk. I have a couple problems of my own."

"What? Is it serious?"

"I always keep my problems to myself. I probably seem so normal to you guys, but I'm just as torn as you are."

"We all have problems, though."

"It's nothing serious. It's more like a secret."

I was really getting impatient. There was no way I could wait until tonight. What could it be? I hope it wasn't that bad, like a deadly disease. I mean, she couldn't get pregnant, so it couldn't be that. What could my friend be hiding?

"Go on, Jessica. I'm listening."

Jessica put her coffee down and walked up to me, taking the baby. "I'm going to lay Mahalia in her bassinet."

Jessica took my baby into the living room where one of her many bassinets were. I waited in the kitchen sitting on the stool. I impatiently tapped my feet on the bars at the bottom of the stool. My hands were tapping the counter. I was pretty nervous of the secret Jessica wanted to tell me. It wasn't before long before she came back into the kitchen. She smiled a bit as she sat in the stool next to me.

"Well, Zaria," she started, "you're very sweet person and I would never do anything to hurt you. I love you like a sister. I'll admit, when you first moved in I hated you, probably 'cause I was jealous. But me and you have been really close lately, and I love everything about you. That's why this secret has been hurting me. Well, I really brought you here. I set this all up for Rahiem and Caddy."

"What?" I was shocked. "But Caddy said he knew I'd come here because of Veronica."

"Well, it was planned. Rahiem was my fiancé."

"You did me dirty like that? What a small fuckin' world."

"I led Caddy to you and I am so sorry. I didn't know you at the time, and you're not a bad person. You never deserved none of this. I mean, Caddy promised he wasn't going to hurt you. He really do love you, girl."

"I'm so confused. You set me up?"

"There's more, and it had nothing to do with Caddy."

"What the hell else did you do?"

Jessica sighed and put her head down. I knew she was angry at what she did. I was angry at what she did. She could've got me killed. What a selfish bitch.

She took a deep breath. "I was also mad that you hooked up with Tony first. I wanted him for myself."

I quickly stood up. "You fucked Tony?!"

"At first I only wanted to get at you. But I am so

sorry I did it."

"In this house?"

"No, Veronica and Trixsy don't know."

"His house?"

"Yes, and hotels, his truck."

"You fuckin' slut!"

"Wait, Azaria, don't even go there. I said I was sorry. You were with Caddy most of the time anyway."

"So you just go fuck my other man. You're the biggest whore I ever met."

"I could've fucked Caddy but I didn't."

I stepped closer into her face. "So you think Caddy would've fucked you?"

"I don't want to take this no further. You're my girl and I still love you."

"Girls don't fuck each other's men. Tony, I'll let him slide, but you think you can get Caddy. Hell no!"

"Why should you love him? He killed Quentin."

"Fuck you!"

I walked away from Jessica and headed toward the living room. I was too mad at her. She really double crossed me. I didn't even get to leave the kitchen when she opened her mouth next. I was shocked at what she blurted out.

"And now I'm pregnant!"

I thought her whorish ass couldn't get pregnant. I didn't think twice when I walked back to toward her and slapped her dead across the face. I knew Jessica was a tough ass and she wasn't just gonna let me slap her. She was quick when she grabbed me by my shirt and pushed me away from her. She pushed me back so hard, I fell over the kitchen table and landed onto the floor. I could tell she didn't wanna fight me, but I didn't give a damn. I wanted to fuck her up. I got back up and swung at her. She backed away and I was swinging at the air.

"Zaria, please calm down," Jessica shouted. "Let's just talk this out."

"Fuck you!" I was still swinging at her and kept missing.

She was running around the island and I was right behind her. She even had her four inch stilettos on. Soon as she fell, I tackled her ass. I was on top of her punching her in the face. She swung at me and busted my lip. She dug her long nails into my neck and scratched my face. I just knew I was going to look fucked up. All the noise we made caused Trixsy to come downstairs. I could hear her yelling at me, then felt someone yank me up. It was Veronica. Trixsy helped Jessica up.

"What's going on with you two?" Veronica yelled at us both.

All you could hear was heavy breathing between me and Jessica. Suddenly, the bitch started crying. I just looked at her, I didn't feel sorry one bit. Her face was really red. Shit, I may have started it, but I knew I was fucked up. I could feel my face burning, my back hurt from that fall, and my knuckles were killing me.

"Your friend's a whore," I finally said.

"Yeah," Veronica agreed, "and?"

"She fucked Tony and now she's pregnant."

Veronica and Trixsy both turned towards Jessica. Trixsy let go of her arm and looked at her with her mouth wide open.

"And her ass told Caddy that I lived here. That's how he found me. She knew him before I did. Her scandalous ass set me up. She was out to get me, too." I looked right into her crying eyes. "And I trusted you all this time with my baby."

"That was then. I didn't really know you. This is why I'm telling you this because I feel bad. I love you, Azaria, and I love Mahalia as my own. I would never hurt her. Please don't hate me. I am so sorry."

I ignored Jessica and turned to Veronica. "Can you watch the baby for a couple of hours? I need to get out."

"Go ahead. I got her."

I walked away from Veronica and walked up to Jessica.

"I don't forgive you and you better stay away from me and my baby!"

I walked away and entered the living room. I kissed my baby and then walked upstairs to my room. I took a quick shower and threw on some blue jeans and a tight green t-shirt that was low cut in the front to show lots of cleavage. I tried to fix my messed up face the best I could.

When I was finish, I grabbed my purse and keys and I was out.

Chapter Thirty

It was 10:30am when I put my car in park and sat there. I took a deep breath before I opened the door and stepped out. Why on earth was I here? I knew I was going crazy. My stupid ass just couldn't stay away.

I rang the doorbell and waited patiently. It was a couple of minutes before the door opened. He stood there almost naked. He wore silk black pajama pants that nearly hung off his ass and you could see his pubic hairs peeking above the silk. He was still as sexy as ever, even if I did hate his ass.

"Sorry to wake you," I said as I looked at his muscular body. "Can I come in?"

Caddy rubbed his eyes as if he couldn't believe I was really there. The biggest smile appeared on his face. He was so excited to see me but his smile left when he noticed my face.

"Damn, baby!" He grabbed my hand and pulled me in. "What happened to you?"

He closed the door behind me and then looked back at my face. He brought his hand up to my face and gently touched it.

"I had a fight with Jessica," I told him.

He dropped his hand and we made eye contact.

He knew why me and Jessica fought, or at least half the reason why.

"You hungry?" he asked. "I'll cook you some breakfast and then we can talk."

"Caddy, I just wanna talk."

"Come on, you need to eat anyway. I know how you get when your all stressed. I know you're stressed."

I sighed, but still followed Caddy into his kitchen. He pulled out a chair for me and I sat down. I watched him go into his freezer and pull out some blueberry waffles. I guess that was what he called cooking. While the waffles were into toaster, he pulled out two glasses and poured some orange juice. He sat one glass in front of me and the other on the opposite end. He walked back to get the waffles and put them on a plate and brought me one with syrup. I just smiled at him.

"Thanks," I said, looking at the waffles.

"I'm glad you came back," Caddy said, taking in a mouth full of waffles. He at me, and I was just sitting there. "Do you forgive me?"

I looked back up at him. "No, not really."

"Then why'd you come back?"

I shrugged my shoulders. I finally picked up the fork and took a bite of my waffle. Caddy just watched me for a minute. Damn, why did I come back? I was nervous, not really scared anymore. I knew he wasn't going to hurt me. Did I want him back though?

"Maybe 'cause I love you," I answered. A smile suddenly appeared on his face again. He reached over the table and put his hands out. I hesitated, but soon my hands were in his. "Do you love me?" I asked him.

"If I didn't love you, I wouldn't be here right now. I know I can't take back that night, but I honestly love you to death. I love you more than Quentin has ever loved you. Quentin was out for himself anyway. You didn't let me tell you the whole story."

"What's that?"

"Quentin didn't care about you. He was doing more than robbing and killing people, he was also a drug dealer which you probably already knew. Well, they had a lead on Quentin and he was close to getting caught up. He was smart with having everything in your name. He hid most of the drugs in your car under the interior.

"No, Quentin wouldn't do that."

"I'm not lying to you. He was trying to make a future with Sonya. It was all about money to Quentin. He was only keeping Sonya because she was going to do a lot of stuff for him, which was going to make him fuckin' rich."

"I just wanna know the truth about one thing."

"What?"

"How'd you find me?"

"I didn't want to get Jessica in trouble, that's why I didn't tell you about her. I told Jessica to get you to move in with them, so she must've told Veronica to call you and offer the deal. That's how I knew you were there." He paused. "I was so selfish at first, and I'll keep apologizing everyday for what I did to you."

I was quiet. I do forgive him. My friends will think I'm crazy, but I forgive him.

"So how'd the fight start?" he asked.

"Jessica fucked Tony."

"She a hoe, so I wouldn't doubt that. I knew his conceited ass wasn't shit!"

"But what made my blood boil was when she said she could've fucked you too."

"Who's that bitch kiddin'? I wouldn't even go there. I knew her for a couple years now and she throws me off."

"After she made that comment, I knew right then that I was still in love with you."

Caddy stood up and walked over to my side of the table. He got on one knee, and grabbed my hand. "Baby, I didn't know I was going to do this, but my heart needs you. I want you and Mahalia to be in my life forever. I want our past behind us and look to the future. I'm sorry, baby, and I'll tell you I'm sorry over and over. I just hope you really forgive me for what I've done and.....let me have your hand in marriage, making you my wife."

I felt a tear trickle down my cheek and Caddy gently wiped it away as we stared into each other's eyes. He waited for my answer and I was speechless. I mean, I already knew my answer, but I was afraid to say it.

"Please, baby," he begged, "say yes."

"Promise me whatever you did the other night, you'll leave all that alone."

"Oh yeah, baby. I promise. That was actually the last of it. I just went to collect my money. That's it."

"Okay."

"So the answer is yes?"

I smiled. "Yes."

Caddy hugged me hard, lifting me right out of my chair. I threw my arms around him and we kissed each other. I cried tears of joy. I didn't want to let go of Caddy. I was so glad this was over with and we could move on with our life.

Epilogue

Me and Mahalia left Veronica, Trixsy, and Jessica. At first they hated the idea, I mean, who wouldn't? Me moving in with my rapist, and boyfriend's murderer, how stupid was I? But it was all worth it. He was the sweetest husband ever. Caddy and I moved to another city where we knew no one and started all over again in Cleveland, Ohio.

We did have one problem in our relationship, Caddy was a real hustler and wanted to try every business possible. Our big money went down quick. Five years later we were living in a five bedroom house that was totally paid off, but we couldn't keep up with the bills. Caddy spent our money on every possible idea he had and they all failed, except one. He had opened up a car business a year and a half ago. It wasn't booming, but we got by.

Every thing was cool until Rahiem found out where Caddy lived and they did one last robbery, where they killed one of the most wealthiest men in South Carolina. Caddy thought he was back on top again until the murder was traced back to him, thanks to Rahiem, who gave his best friend up.

I remember the day crystal clear. Mahalia was six. We were in the kitchen one morning eating breakfast and Caddy was still asleep. From out of nowhere, here comes the police breaking down all the doors. I didn't have time to grab Mahalia and get away. A cop grabbed her and another grabbed me and more went upstairs. I was going crazy as Mahalia was crying and screaming my name. I thought they were hurting her. I tried my best to break loose from the two officers that held tight onto me. Next thing I saw was Caddy being escorted in handcuffs to the front door and outside. They took him right from bed to the police station. I was devastated.

They got him for the murder charges but and not the robbery. I thought I'd die when they sentenced him thirty years in a federal prison. I knew I lost him forever.

I didn't have anyone else, not even my friends. We all fell out after I married Caddy. Me and Jessica been through, even after she got the abortion I still didn't talk to her. Trixsy got married to some guy name David and they were happy I suppose.

Veronica quit stripping a while ago. She was into something more serious and dangerous. She met the wrong guy and he got her into prostitution and drugs. Her new boyfriend, Darnell, was actually her pimp and moved her to Atlantic City. When I got my life together, I was going to go get my friend and save her. I knew she didn't want to be doing that.

Chari was just like Jessica, and now she was the back stabbing bitch. I heard she was fucking with Tony. They were all whores. Tony didn't seem that way at first, I was surprised.

I roll alone. I live in this big house with my daughter and I write Caddy everyday and see him once a week. He still has the best lawyer ever and I hope he got my baby out. I don't care how long it takes, I will wait for my man!

Printed in the United States
141223LV00002B/1/P

9 780982 053058